The Riven

Ghost Wolf Series, Book 2

T. L. Riffey

Publishing Coordinator – Sharon Kizziah-Holmes

Paperback-Press
an imprint of A & S Publishing
Paperback Press, LLC.

ISBN -13: 978-1-956806-58-8

DEDICATION

For the Kumpanija and Shavora out there
May you find your Ruv and She'endra/e

PROLOGUE

Outside the sun had started to rise but the only sound in the dark room was a rhythmic drip, drip. Sunlight began to peek around the closed curtains as the sun rose higher and the alarm went off but there was still no movement in the room. Minutes went by and the sunlight advanced a bit more into the room. It struck something on the carpet and glistened.

Noise like boots on wood came from outside the closed door, then a hard knock sounded on its wood surface.

"This is the police! Are you alright?" A voice called from the other side.

Seconds passed in silence, then the doorknob moved, and the door was flung open. Two uniformed policemen leaned in and just as quickly jerked back. The younger of the two threw up beside the door while the older man hit his radio and called it in.

The light from the hallway skylight revealed the grisly scene in all its horrific glory. What had once been two human beings lay open on the bed like some medical students' cadavers. Blood splattered the bed and the floor around it, but all the walls except one was clean. Sprawled across that wall written in blood were five strange words and a question mark.

Kaj si le Ratta Lil?

What it meant the older uniform officer didn't know but this was no longer his headache. The detectives would come and take over, then he and his partner would be relegated to guards. He moved to help his partner down the stairs so they could wait by the front door for the others to arrive, the alarm echoing behind them.

CHAPTER 1

Detective John Hanlan flipped the radio station but the new one had Christmas music as well. It wasn't even Thanksgiving yet. Granted it was in a few days but, still, it was way too early for Christmas songs.

"I thought you humans enjoyed this season," Tom Canin, his partner, said from the passenger seat, his cognac eyes gleaming with amusement.

"It's like they forget Thanksgiving. Just because it's not commercially viable the stores skip right over it. As soon as Halloween is over, BAM— Christmas."

Before Canin could say anything to Hanlan's rant his cell phone rang. He pulled it out of his jacket's inner pocket, saw it was their captain, and hit the speaker button. "Canin."

"Detective, are you and Hanlan on your way to the station?"

"Yes, Ma'am," he answered with a glance at Hanlan.

"You need to detour to 425 Shadow Lane, Croft Manor. Howell and Deneque will brief you at the scene." The phone went dead at the last word.

Hanlan made a left turn and changed direction, driving toward the address given.

Canin returned his phone to his suit jacket pocket. "At least it's not Raven Manor," he told his grim-faced partner.

"Across the street."

They remained silent for the rest of the drive, neither wanting to think about the case that had brought them together, but Hanlan's mind went there anyway.

A few days before Halloween, the affluent Graves' had been murdered and the captain had assigned Hanlan to get it closed fast. They had been killed in a strange way and in a peculiar residence, leading Hanlan to discover a hidden world. A world his new partner was a part of. And which they were both now involved in.

Hanlan pulled in through the open wooden gate and parked behind the M.E.'s van in the circular drive. He sat there a minute and looked at the Manor.

Raven Manor had been Gothic in appearance, but Croft Manor looked like a fairy tale castle, complete with stone turrets, tall thin windows, and stout wood front door. There was even a wide circle of blue stones to represent the moat that disappeared around the building. The building's stone was reflecting the morning sun and, if it wasn't for the police cars and M.E. van, the Manor would be the picture of English serenity with its manicured lawn and gardens.

"Are you coming?" Canin had gotten out of the car but had paused when Hanlan hadn't followed.

"Yeah." Hanlan got out and they both headed for the half-open front door.

Just inside the door a young, uniformed officer waited. Past him an ornate staircase lead upwards, then split in half heading in opposite directions. Downstairs to their left a formal dining room lay and to the right the formal living room.

Hanlan raised an eyebrow and the uniform pointed up and to the left.

"Come on up," came Howell's voice from above as his head briefly appeared over the railing.

The detectives went up and took the left fork, arriving at the landing moments later. Their fellow detectives Howell and Deneque were there waiting as were two morgue assistants with a stretcher and two body bags.

"Two victims., John and Sara Ruthridge." Howell was the speaker as normal for the other detective pair. "He was an Investment Banker and she seemed to shop for a living. Paperboy saw the door open and told the neighbor Mr. Halcome who called 911. The uniforms showed up and cleared the downstairs before coming up here. The door was closed so they announced themselves, then opened the door."

"One of them must be a rookie," Hanlan said, gesturing to the mess by the door.

"First week." Howell nodded. "CSU gave him a talking to."

Hanlan grunted.

"I almost lost mine," Deneque said quietly.

"I thought I heard your voice." A young woman stuck her head out the door. "They said you'd be taking over, and I know you like to look things over before I remove the bodies, so I waited."

"Doctor Brennon." Hanlan gave her a nod. "What can you tell me so far?"

"Whomever did this has a working knowledge of human anatomy. Can't tell you much more until after I do my autopsy."

"Alright. Thanks."

She nodded and ducked back inside.

"CSU inside?" Hanlan asked Howell.

"Waiting on you," Howell told him.

Hanlan took a deep breath and arranged his face into a neutral expression before he and Canin moved to the bedroom door. They took a step inside and stop to survey the room. Hanlan had seen horrendous murder scenes in his years as a homicide detective but that hadn't prepared him for the scene before him. He could feel the roil of Canin's emotions as well at the sight. It wasn't the most gruesome but there was something about it that sent shivers up his spine. Perhaps it was the eerie smiles etched into the victims' faces or the naked bloody footprints that marred the carpet. Maybe it was even the wanton carving and removal of the organs.

But he knew it was really the words written in blood on the one wall.

Where is the blood book?

Brennon and a CSU tech were standing off to the side and Hanlan snapped a question off at the CSU tech. "Have you examined the footprints?"

"Yes." He nodded. "Too small to be a man's. At least not an average size man's. I made a print. Once I'm back at the lab I can tell more."

Hanlan nodded before looking over the scene again. He spotted the knife lying between the bed and the en-suite, the sunlight from the window above the headboard that peeked out of the curtains reflecting off its blade. It was a wicked-looking thing, with a serrated edge on one side and what looked like a razor-sharp edge on the other. The bloody footprints led into the en-suite, and he could hear movement within, another CSU tech no doubt. He had seen all he needed to. "I'm done," he told Brennon and the tech.

The CSU tech nodded and pulled an evidence bag from his case before stepping carefully in his booties toward the knife.

As Hanlan and Canin turned to leave, Brennon called to them to wait. They paused and looked at her.

"I'll have the report to you as soon as I can," she told them.

Hanlan nodded but didn't say anything, just waited. He knew there was something else on her mind.

"Fall of 1989. The Laney Murders."

"How do you know about them?" Canin asked.

"You're not old enough to have been a M.E. then."

"I've read all the old unsolved cases my office handled in the past." She shrugged. "I'm a murder groupie. Why do you think I became a M.E.?" she added.

"I'll look into it," Hanlan promised.

"Good. When can my assistants take the bodies without messing your crime scene up?" she asked the CSU tech, dismissing the detectives from her mind.

The two of them exited the bedroom and joined Howell and Deneque a few feet away on the landing.

"We have uniforms canvasing the neighborhood, but it's unlikely they'll find anything. These homes are just far enough apart that unless you're paying attention or lucky you don't see or hear much. And most people would have been asleep."

"Depending on when it happened. The front door didn't look jimmied. What about the back?" Hanlan asked.

"Locked tight. And nothing seems out of place downstairs. But not so up here."

Hanlan raised an eyebrow.

Howell turned and led the way around the landing to one of the other open doors. He gestured for Hanlan to look in.

Stepping up, Hanlan leaned in and whistled. This room had obviously been a library. The bookcases were empty though because every single book was thrown about the floor, and a display case was lying broken near the back wall. A CSU tech was dusting the display case for fingerprints and Hanlan asked,

"Can you bag the contents of the rolltop for me?"

It was the only thing still standing intact as even the chairs and couch had been overturned.

"Sure. I'll drop them off after I get back to the lab."

"Thanks." Hanlan ducked back out. "Whomever the killer is he or she was obviously looking for either a book or something inside one."

"The neighbor said Mr. Ruthridge was a book collector and had just come back from a book auction at Barrington's last night."

"Maybe the killer followed him home."

"Could be." Howell paused. "The captain said we were to work with you on this case. She wants it solved fast. Before the rumors get out of hand."

"Figured. You two take his workplace. Canin and I will follow up at Barrington's this morning. We'll get together after lunch to exchange notes."

"Sounds good."

The four of them headed downstairs. Howell and Deneque stopped at the bottom of the stairs but Hanlan and Canin continued on and out the door. They didn't speak until they were safely out of earshot in the car.

"What are the odds that this 'blood book' is the Lexicon?" Hanlan demanded of Canin.

"High." Canin pulled out his cell and tapped on it. "I'm leaving a text for Phuro."

"Good." Hanlan wanted to talk to the Ruv Elder himself. "Is there a new player or do you think Lupo is playing a game with us?"

"I don't know." Canin shook his head as he returned his phone to his jacket pocket. "And we can't dismiss the Trust."

"No. I wouldn't put this past Cowen." Hanlan started the vehicle and drove away from the manor.

The Alsena Historical Society and Trust was a cover for the local Ruv Hunters. Jennifer Cowen was the Assistant Director and a seasoned Hunter. She wouldn't think twice about killing people if it got her her way of the Directorship. That, Hanlan was sure of. He had only met her the once, but she had made an impression on him, and his gut was rarely wrong. She gave him the same feeling as most murderers did.

"I thought Barrington's sold fancy art pieces and furniture." Canin's voice broke into Hanlan's thoughts. "Not books."

"Depends upon the book. If it's rare or old they auction it off like the others."

"Huh."

Hanlan knew Canin wasn't much of a book reader, he spent most of their down time watching TV or on his phone. But Hanlan liked to curl up on the sofa with a book or his eReader, and not just with fiction either. He's read many a scientific article and paper on crime. Hanlan wasn't a 'dumb cop' by any means. In today's Force you couldn't be and be a good cop.

Canin had been born and bred an enforcer, the Ruv equivalent of a cop but with different rules and morals. That he had become a cop in the human world showed that he had a moral compass which aligned at least partially with human law.

Slowing, Hanlan turned into Park Central Square East, part of the street that 'encircled' Alsena's main park though it was actually rectangular. Barrington's was across the street from the park which meant parking was an exercise in frustration if you were not there for one of their auctions. There was no parking on the street itself and only a small parking lot half-way down between two businesses. However, Barrington's had underground parking. It had once been a three-story apartment building before it had been transformed into a prestigious auction house.

He drove into the garage and stopped at the gate, pulling out his badge wallet from his suit's inner jacket pocket with his free hand.

"Can I help you?" The guard leaned his head out of the small guard booth as he spoke.

"I'm Detective Hanlan and this is my partner Detective Canin." Hanlan held up his badge for the man to see. "We need to talk to someone about last night's auction."

The guard studied the badge for a moment, then pressed a button on the desktop in front of him, causing the gate to open. "I'll call up and someone will meet you inside. Park anywhere."

Hanlan nodded and drove forward, slipping his badge back in his pocket. Arrows pointed toward the main garage's building entrance, and he parked as close as possible to it.

Both detectives got out of the car and headed toward the door.

Hanlan didn't know if he should hope for a lead or not here. They didn't want anything leading toward the Lexicon, but they needed to find the killer before any other murders could happen. A bit of a quandary.

Canin opened the door and the detectives stepped inside.

CHAPTER 2

The lobby was large.

Barrington's had left the mailboxes and the lobby desk, but they had obviously put in the window and glass front door, though it was beautifully done. The tiled floor was also no doubt new as most apartment buildings' lobbies were carpeted and the seating area had surely been added. Hanlan was impressed.

A woman and a uniformed man stood behind the desk and that was where the detectives headed. As they came closer, the long-haired woman moved out from behind the desk and approached them with her hand out. "Detectives, I'm Jami Rose, one of the Curators here."

"Curator?" Hanlan asked as he shook her hand.

Rose shook Canin's hand and gave him a nod as she answered. "It's a fancy name for those of us who are Jacks-of-all-Trades. I do a little bit of everything."

"I see. Can you talk to us about last night's auction?"

"Certainly. Let's go to one of the conference rooms." She gestured toward the stairs.

"I don't mean to be too nosy but how do you get your furniture moved around here?" Canin asked as they all headed toward the stairway.

"We have a freight elevator in the back that goes from the top floor to the garage."

"Ah."

Rose led the way up one floor and half-way down the hallway to a door marked with a large 'C1'. She opened the door and gestured for them to enter, then followed them in when they did.

A large oval glass table dominated the room with pine wood chairs. At the rear of the room was a media center and two white boards. There was no windows, but the overheads were bright and lit the room well.

After making sure the door was closed, Rose moved to the head of the table and sat down. She gestured for the detectives to sit before she spoke. "What do you need to know, Detectives?"

"Mr. Ruthridge was supposedly here last night."

"Indeed he was," she told Hanlan. "He bid on several collections."

"Was there a heated bidding on any of them, especially any he won?"

"Hmm. The last. He won but it was fast and

furious between him and another bidder."

"Who was the other bidder?"

"Never seen her before so I don't know her name without looking it up."

"Could you?"

"This is a gray area. I probably should have you get a subpoena. My bosses will probably be upset with me for talking this much."

Hanlan raised an eyebrow.

"But Shavora should be respected," she answered his unspoken question.

"You're Roma?" he blurted out. She was as nearly light-skinned as the almost albino Canin.

"No, Ruv." Her hazel eyes twinkled with amusement.

"But your eyes..."

"The odd human here and there, but I am Ruv."

Before either Hanlan or Canin could speak, the door opened, and an older bald man stepped inside. "Jami."

"Mr. Barrington," Rose said smoothly. "these detectives wanted to meet you and talk about last night's auction. I told them they would probably need a subpoena for any information. But they still wanted to meet you."

Hanlan and Canin both got up as she talked, then Hanlan stepped forward and offered his hand. "Indeed, we did. We were hoping you'd be more accommodating when we tell you that Mr. Ruthridge was killed last night after attending your auction."

Mr. Barrington accepted Hanlan's hand but shook his head. "While I'm sorry to hear that, I'm afraid I must insist on a subpoena. Our records are confidential."

"All right. We or some of our colleagues will be back with that subpoena."

"Ms. Rose will see you out." Barrington turned on his heel and left as Rose arose from her chair.

"Sorry for throwing you under the bus."

"I understand." And Hanlan did. Barrington gave off the same bad vibes as Deneque's father did. Perhaps Barrington was a Hunter too.

Rose gestured them towards the door and the three of them exited the room. She led the way back downstairs and stopped at the bottom of the stairs. "You can take it from here I'm sure."

"One more question if you will," Hanlan said. "The collection he bought where'd it come from?"

She glanced at the guard at the desk, then up the stairs before speaking. "The Alsena Historical Society and Trust brought them here, but the books were all stamped with 'From the Graves Estate'."

The detectives glanced at each other, then Hanlan told her, "Thank you for your assistance."

Rose nodded and, turning, went back up the stairs.

Both of the detectives headed for the garage door, keeping silent as they mulled over what they had learned. Once in the garage, they went to the car and got in before speaking.

"Did you know she was Ruv?" Hanlan asked Canin.

"She smells like one, but like you said her eyes are not."

"Is she a member of the city Pack?"

"I don't know. You can ask Phuro." Canin had pulled out his phone and was looking at it. "He wants to meet us this afternoon at the library."

Hanlan grunted, then started the car and headed toward the gate.

As Hanlan drove, Canin slipped his phone back in his jacket pocket and remained silent until they exited onto the street. "How we going to handle this? You mentioned our colleagues, meaning Howell and Deneque."

"I'll write it up, but they can see the judge and serve it while we talk with Phuro."

"And afterwards?"

"We'll take it as it comes."

The precinct building loomed up ahead. It was a five-story stone goliath with the crime lab in the two underground floors. A grant had been allocated to the city twenty years ago for a new crime lab and the Mayor had lobbied to combine the proposal of a new police station for this district with the allocated crime lab. The Brass had put in their own two cents as well about new offices for them. Thus this building and a big plaque in the main lobby.

Hanlan headed to the parking lot in the back and pulled into one of the slots marked "Detective". They weren't marked personally but he usually parked in this one down a ways from the back stairs.

Both of the detectives got out of the car and jogged up the main back steps. Once inside there were elevators and stairs to the right, a double door to the front, and a caged window with a cage door beside it to the left. An older man could be seen seated at a desk just inside through the window and the detectives headed over.

"Jack," Hanlan called softly.

The older man stood and came up to the window. His salt and pepper hair and beard were neatly trimmed and his uniform crisp but loose on his mediumly built frame. "John. Canin."

Hanlan had known Jack Reach since his first month in Homicide when he had arrived ten years ago. Jack was the guardian of files and evidence boxes. And he took his job very seriously. Nothing left his domain without a signature. Late nights had led to their meeting and they had hit it off from day one. Hanlan now considered him a good friend, but he was still wary of him as he used to be a Hunter though he had only learned of that recently.

"I need a file," Hanlan told him. "1989. Laney Murders."

"I'll get it to you this afternoon."

Hanlan nodded, then asked, "How you liking day shift?"

"Hate it. But they reorganized and said a night supervisor isn't needed so Jameson's cut down to just my off-days and vacation or sick days and I'm day shift."

"Sorry."

Reach sighed. "I'll get used to it. Go on now and let me get back to my paperwork. I won't forget the file."

"Thanks," Hanlan said before he and Canin headed for the elevator.

They took it up to the fourth floor where the Homicide Division was. Major Case and Robbery shared the floor as well some of the higher-ups that were banished from the rest of the Brass on the second floor.

Both of them stepped off the elevator when the doors opened and headed down the hall toward the double wood doors that signified the Homicide Division's bullpen. When they got to the doors, they shoved their way through and headed to the left toward their desks.

Hanlan noticed their captain was waiting for them there. He didn't know if that was good or bad.

The African-American woman stood silent until they both sat at their desks. "I got a call from the Mayor."

"Not the Chief?"

"Him too. But the Mayor wanted to personally tell me how important it is to solve this case. It seems Ruthridge was his personal banker and friend."

"Ah."

"I told him I had my best detectives on the case. Don't make me a liar, gentlemen."

Hanlan nodded and watched her head back to her office before turning to Canin. "Do the initial report. I'm going to get to work on the subpoena. Everything needs to be by the book and triple checked."

Canin nodded and got to work on his computer while Hanlan turned to his. They worked on their assignments diligently, the silence around their desks only broken by the sound of their typing and the murmur of the other detectives working their own cases.

A throat clearing interrupted their concentration and they both surfaced to see Howell and Deneque standing at Hanlan's desk. Hanlan glanced at the clock to see it was close to lunch time. He hated doing warrants or subpoenas. They were time-suckers.

"We still on for meeting after lunch?" Howell asked.

"Yeah." He glanced over the form on the screen, then hit the print button. "Then you'll be serving a subpoena at Barrington's while Canin and I follow up on something."

"Sounds like you had an interesting time there." Howell raised an eyebrow.

Hanlan grunted. "Grab the form and see Judge Peterson before lunch. We'll meet at 1 p.m."

"Right. See you then." Howell and Deneque hurried away toward the printer by the front door.

"You almost done?" Hanlan asked Canin.

"Yeah. I was doing the notes."

"Let's get out of here." Hanlan stood and stretched before pushing his chair under the desk.

"I'm ready for lunch." Canin stood as well, pushing his own chair under his desk.

Both of them turned and headed toward the doors, eager to leave everything behind for a while.

CHAPTER 3

When Hanlan and Canin came back from lunch at Joey's, the local cop diner, they took the back elevator to the fourth floor. But instead of going in the bullpen they headed for the conference room just down the hall from the elevator.

The conference room was small but cozy with a TV cabinet at the front of the room. Canin planted his butt on the oval table while Hanlan pulled out a chair and sat. Most of the detectives used this room for strategic meetings or to view DVD or VHS evidence. The Brass used the large conference room on the second floor, even the ones exiled to this floor.

Howell and Deneque entered and grabbed a

chair, facing Hanlan.

Canin slid into a chair beside his partner.

"Did you get the subpoena?" Hanlan asked as soon as everyone was settled.

"Yep." Howell patted his suit's jacket pocket. "Judge Peterson sure loves your thoroughness."

Hanlan made a face, then asked, "Did you read it?"

"I skimmed it. The list of participants could be large."

"Probably. But we're interested in a woman that bet against him in the last auction of books brought in by the Alsena Historical Society and Trust. We have reason to believe she was upset about losing."

"You think he was carved up like that over some books?" Howell's voice and face was skeptical.

"You saw the library."

"It was important to the killer," Deneque said quietly. "Whatever it is. Doesn't matter if we agree or not."

"You're right," Howell agreed with a sigh.

"So how was your morning?" Hanlan asked them, changing the subject slightly.

"About as productive as yours. His boss said he had no enemies and was one of their best. No real losses, just the normal up and downs. But he did say Ruthridge took a personal day two days ago. He didn't know why."

"Follow up on that if you can."

"Okay." Howell gave him a nod. "He also claimed confidentiality towards Ruthridge's client list."

"I wouldn't doubt it. The Mayor called the

captain."

Howell made a face. "Great."

"So everything in triplicate."

"Right." Howell and Deneque stood. "Anything else we need to know?"

"Not right now."

"Then we'll go serve this subpoena. Meet back in the bullpen later?"

Hanlan nodded and the other two detectives left.

"Mr. Barrington is going to know Rose said something to us when he reads the subpoena."

"No, he won't. That's why I asked for a list of all the participants. We'll pick out the women and run down which she is through other channels."

"One of the others might know who the bidder was."

"Yep."

Canin gave him an irritated look.

Hanlan smiled and stood. "Let's go see Phuro, Partner."

Sighing, Canin stood as well.

They pushed their chairs back under the table, then headed out the door. Once in the hallway, they turned and moved to the back elevator. They rode down in silence.

Reach wasn't at his desk, so they continued on and out the back door. When they reached the car, they got in and Hanlan drove out of the parking lot.

Phuro or Professor Ulven as he was known to humans was the city Pack's Alpha. He was also the guardian of the Lexicon right now. It was somewhat cleverly stashed at the Carnegie branch of the city's library which was where they were now headed.

With shortcuts, it didn't take Hanlan long to get to the library. The gray stone two story building wasn't huge, and they had come in the side parking lot, so it took but a minute for Hanlan to follow it around to the back. Along part of the back there was a wrought iron fence and that was where Hanlan directed the car. He parked in front of the fence and the detectives got out. They rounded the fence and went down the ramp it partially enclosed. Knocking on the door at the bottom, they waited.

The door opened minutes later to reveal an old man. He was dressed in linen pants and a colorful peasant shirt. He ushered them in and locked the door behind them before hurrying them through a second door into a room full of half-shelves and books.

Hanlan glanced over to a special glass and wood display case, reassuring himself that the Lexicon was still there, before looking at the old man. "Phuro."

"I don't think your killer is a Hunter," Phuro stated right off. "Or a Shilmulo. Even a rogue Ruv won't waste blood like that."

Hanlan glanced at Canin with a raised eyebrow before returning his attention to Phuro. "Then why was that message sprawled across the wall?"

"Canin said it was in the Common Tongue?" Phuro asked, a thoughtful look on his face.

The Ruv elder wasn't answering his question, Hanlan noted but replied to Phuro's question anyway. "A version of Romani, yes."

"Not all of the Roma were welcoming. An individual here and there, sometimes a whole family, did not like us, considered us prastlo--unclean. They usually ended up pikie—exiled by the Phuro, Elders. But I know some of them came together and formed their own packs."

"You think this killer may be one of them?"

"It is something to keep in mind." Phuro paused as a young woman came over to them from the archway on their left. "You need something, Ms. Gayl?"

She nervously fiddled with her glasses around her neck, her cognac eyes going from Hanlan to Phuro. "You wanted me to remind you about Professor Simpson coming in today, Professor Ulven."

"Quite right, my dear. I'm almost finished here."

Gayl gave him a nod, then scurried away back to her desk through the archway.

Hanlan watched her leave, then turned his attention back to Phuro and raised an eyebrow.

"She's skittish around others, humans especially unless they're academics." Phuro shrugged. "But she loves books and researching."

"Huh." Hanlan shook his head to clear it of the mousy Ruv, then said, "That reminds me. We met a Ruv today at Barrington's. Jami Rose. Is she a member of your city Pack?"

"Jami Rose. No." Phuro frowned. Before he could say anything else, voices came from through the archway, and he gestured them toward the door. "You need to leave. I'll get in touch with you soon."

Hanlan nodded, then both of the detectives followed Phuro until he shoved them outside and closed the second door behind them. They waited until they heard Phuro lock the door, then headed up the ramp to the parking lot.

"Who's this Professor Simpson?" Hanlan asked as they got into the car. "Phuro was sure in a hurry to make sure he didn't see us."

"One of Director Deneque's researchers. He's also a Chair at the University."

"Ah." Hanlan drove out of the parking lot and headed toward his station. "Better safe than sorry."

"Yeah."

They rode the rest of the way in silence. Once at the station, Hanlan parked in his usual spot in back and they got out of the car. They jogged up the stairs and went inside. Reach still wasn't at his desk so they continued on into the elevator and went up to the fourth floor. When they got to the bullpen, they saw that Howell and Deneque weren't there yet, so they headed to their desks.

Two large paper evidence bags were sitting on Hanlan's desk.

"Contents of the rolltop in the library of Croft Manor," Hanlan said at Canin's raised eyebrow. They both sat down before Hanlan slid one of the bags closer and opened it. He emptied it on his desk and set the bag on the floor beside him.

"Hand me the other one."

Hanlan tossed the surprisingly light bag on Canin's desk, then returned his attention to the miscellaneous stuff on his own. Pencils, pens, and paperclips went back into the bag, but he looked over every paper article he found before putting it back in the bag. He didn't find anything probative, so he closed the bag and set it in his bottom drawer before looking toward Canin.

There were a couple of piles on Canin's desk, and he was staring at something that looked like an invoice.

"What's that?" he asked Canin.

"The invoice from last night's auction." He handed it over the desk to Hanlan, then settled back in his chair. "There's several here from this year. Also some advertisements and letters about other sales featuring antique books. A few of them are circled."

"We can have Howell and Deneque run them down," Hanlan said absently as he looked over the invoice. "This just says he bought the lot, no list of the books. That's not usual for Barrington's."

"Perhaps they were doing it as a favor to the Trust."

"Hmm." He pulled an evidence bag from his drawer and slipped the invoice inside. "Anything else interesting?"

"No." Canin shook his head as he laid down his pen, then ripped off a piece of paper. "Here's the list of the circled auctions."

Hanlan reached over and grabbed the paper Canin was extending. He set it on his desk. "I wonder what's taking them so long with Barrington."

Before Canin could say anything, Howell and Deneque swept in and stopped at Hanlan's desk. Deneque was frowning and Howell had a scowl on his face.

"What happened?" Hanlan asked.

"Barrington made us wait until his lawyer got

there first of all. Then both of them started in saying they would talk with their good friend Director Deneque about this inconvenience and that he's the one we should be harassing as last night's auction proceeds were for the Trust."

"The whole auction's proceeds?"

"That's what Barrington said."

Hanlan glanced over at Canin, then returned his attention to Howell. "But he gave up the list?"

"Grudgingly." Howell handed Hanlan a folded sheet of paper. "Twenty names but only five are women according to Barrington."

Laying that paper down, he picked up the torn sheet and handed it to Howell. "We need you to run these down. See if Ruthridge had any trouble at any of them."

"More auction houses?"

"Yep."

Howell made a face as he took the sheet of paper.

"You can wait until tomorrow if you'd rather."

"We'll look them up right now so we can start tomorrow morning fresh."

Hanlan nodded and watched them head off toward their desks before turning to Canin. "Good friend Director Deneque, ay?"

Canin just grunted.

"Let's see who our ladies are." Hanlan unfolded the paper list and ran a finger down it. "Ivana Novik, Charity Haul, Kezia Vadoma, Christy..."

"Wait. Kezia Vadoma."

Hanlan looked up at the tone in Canin's voice. It was unsteady. "Canin?"

"Eighty-seven years ago a Roma with the name Vadoma was exiled for killing the rest of her family and attempting to kill a Ruv. She was one of those that Phuro spoke of. The reason she wasn't killed outright though by the Ruv was because she was pregnant. She escaped the next night, probably with help, and was never seen again."

"Your old territory?"

"Yeah."

Hanlan typed the name into his computer but came up empty. "No sheet. At least not under that name. Let's just try Kezia and see what comes up." He tapped the enter button and sighed. "Five Kezia's listed as residing in Alsena."

"Not too bad."

"I was hoping it was unusual enough to be less." He hit the print button. "Want to get the papers?"

Canin stood, then went to retrieve the printouts. He was back in a few minutes but didn't hand the papers to Hanlan as he was looking them over himself.

"Well?"

"Kezia James and Kezia Stein." He handed over their papers while tossing the others to his desk. "Both with shoplifting, petty theft and fraud. A lot of the pikie turn to crime though some of the Roma have too. Life can be harsh."

"Ain't that the truth." Hanlan set the papers on his desk and his eyes happen to fall on the auction list. "Well, well."

"What?"

"Guess who the fifth female is?"

Canin merely raised an eyebrow.

"Julia Lupo."

CHAPTER 4

"On that note, I think it's time to leave." Canin gestured to the clock, then around the nearly empty bullpen. "I don't think we can do anything else tonight."

Hanlan nodded and stood, pushing his chair under his desk.

"And we need to pick up the Laney file before Reach leaves." Canin slid his own chair under his own desk.

"He won't leave until he gives me the file." Hanlan led the way out of the bullpen. "He just won't put in any overtime for it."

They got in the elevator and rode down in silence. Reach was indeed still sitting at his desk when they got off the elevator but stood up and came over to the window with a thick file when they approached. He slid a clipboard through the slot with a pen.

Hanlan dutifully signed it, noted that Reach had put the time down as an hour ago, then slid it back through the slot. He accepted the file Reach slid him. "Thanks, Jack."

Reach nodded and hung the clipboard back under the window desk area.

The two detectives headed out and hurried down the stairs. They got in the car and Hanlan drove out into the street.

"Want to stop at Chickie's?" Hanlan asked Canin.

"No. I thawed some soup from the freezer."

Canin made good soup, ironically called Gypsy Soup. He always cooked a big pot when he made it and froze some for when they didn't feel like take-out or Canin didn't feel like cooking. Hanlan could burn water, but Canin was a fair cook, when he wanted to be.

Hanlan lived about twenty minutes from the station on a good traffic day, but morning and evening traffic were almost always bad. He flipped the radio on, then off as soon as the first Christmas song blared from the speakers. Silence was preferable to him.

Canin flashed him a smile but remained quiet.

The street Hanlan turned into had a row of stone townhouses, most with a basement apartment. This was an older neighborhood, but the homeowners were all young professionals. Converted basement meant money coming in that they could spend.

He drove around back of the one on the end and parked in his slot. When he had looked for apartments ten years ago he had lucked out. This basement apartment had just come up to rent the day he had looked at the basement apartment next door. The apartment was outstanding, and he had immediately paid the deposit, though he'd had to eat cheaply for a month.

Hanlan had loved the place, but it hadn't become a home until Canin had moved in after Halloween. It just felt different with Canin there.

He grabbed the file before he and Canin slid out of the sedan and headed to the stairway next to the main back stairs. There was a front and a back entrance while most had only one. They hurried down the stairs and ducked into the lighted covered entry. With a flick of the key, the door opened and both of them stepped inside.

Closing and locking the door behind them, Hanlan glanced around. The entryway was small with hooks beside the door holding their coats and an archway about six feet in front of them. Nothing seemed to be disturbed. He headed through the archway into the kitchen/living area, following Canin. This area took up half the space of the apartment while the two bedrooms and bath filled the rest.

Canin stopped in the kitchen, but Hanlan stepped past him into the living room and headed toward the three doors on the wall to the left. He glanced in the archway leading to the front door to check for mail but didn't see any telltale whiteness.

As he passed the coffee table he dropped the file

there and continued on to the right-hand door. It was his bedroom, and he took off his suit jacket, hanging it on the bed's foot board as he moved to the open door leading to the bathroom between the two bedrooms.

He made a pit stop and washed his hands before going back into the main area through the bathroom door. Hanlan sat down on the couch and leaned over the coffee table, opening the file. The two crime scene photos attached to the file showed a panorama almost identical to what he had seen at Croft Manor. There were no words sprawled across the wall, but there were two symbols, symbols that looked familiar.

Canin came in with a tray which he sat on the coffee table over the file.

Hanlan just sighed and grabbed a bowl off the tray. His partner was a mother-hen when it came to his companion—his Shavora's health. No more skipped meals or late nights if Canin could help it.

The Ruv sat down next to him and grabbed his own bowl. They ate in silence.

After finishing his soup, Hanlan set the bowl down on the tray and grabbed the glass of water. He drank down half the glass, then set it back on the tray. "Coffee?"

"Yes." Canin nodded as he stood. He set his own bowl down before picking up the tray. "I'll be back in a minute."

Hanlan turned his attention back to the file. The photographs of the symbols were a bit blurry, but he was sure those symbols came from the Lexicon. They weren't the symbols from its cover, but that first page had those symbols he was almost positive.

Canin held the coffee mug in front of Hanlan's eyes, breaking his concentration.

"Thanks." Hanlan grabbed the mug and took a sip before handing a photo of the symbols to Canin. "What do you think of this?"

Ignoring the photo for a moment, Canin sat down beside Hanlan on the couch. He set his own mug down on the coffee table, then looked at the photograph. "It's a bit grainy."

Hanlan merely raised an eyebrow.

Canin sighed, then laid the photograph down on the coffee table. "It does look like the symbols from the Lexicon." He used his phone to snap a pic of the photo, then sent a text. "There. I sent it to Phuro."

"Good." Hanlan went through the file one-handed as he slowly sipped his coffee and Canin sat quietly messing with his phone. By the time he had drank the last of his coffee, Hanlan had finished the file. He set the mug down on the coffee table next to Canin's cup, then leaned back and looked at his partner.

Raising his eyes, Canin slipped his phone into his jacket pocket and turned his attention to Hanlan.

"Nick and Nora Laney were booksellers and they had just come back from a buying trip overseas."

"Interesting that."

"What I find even more interesting was that they had had their books shipped to Barrington's. The old location, of course. Barrington's didn't move to Park Central until a year after I came."

"An employee, you think?"

"A possibility. We'll have to get another

subpoena for his records."

"And the murders themselves?"

"On the face of it they look similar, but we'll have to wait on the autopsy report."

"Was their shop rifled?" Canin asked next. "Or their home?"

"Only the storage room of the shop. They lived in an apartment above the store. All the crates were split open, and the books were thrown about the room."

"What did the investigating detectives think?"

"Only the lead detective left any notes, and he didn't have much in there. This was before they instituted the note system we have today."

"So nothing probative?" Canin frowned.

"Hardly any leads and those they did have were dead ends. Or at least seem to be. He was suspicious of Mr. Barrington but nothing concrete."

"The Mr. Barrington we met?"

"The very same. His father had just retired, and Barrington had only been the boss for a few months. The detective was sure he was hiding something though."

"Perhaps his connection to the Trust. He may have been a new recruit back then."

"Or a new patron with inside knowledge."

"Hmm." Canin was frowning again.

Hanlan glanced at his watch, then leaned forward and picked up the remote. He hit the power button and the TV flashed on, showing the weather.

"What's our game plan for tomorrow?" Canin asked him.

"I'm going to call Dr. Brennon first thing to ask

her to run an extended tox panel," Hanlan told him, keeping his eyes on the TV. "Then I'm working on that subpoena for Barrington's employee records. Howell and Deneque can serve it after Judge Peterson signs it."

"And what am I supposed to be doing while you do the lion's share?"

"Making an appointment with Ms. Lupo for a talk about her night at Barrington's." Hanlan felt Canin's amusement at the mutual animosity between him and Lupo. She was Shilmulo. But there was a method to her madness and that was all that the other Ruv saw. Canin was wary around her for his sake but didn't really think her Shilmulo.

"Then?"

"Updating the notes with this information. With a bit of creative license, of course, about the symbols."

"They're occult symbols, of course."

Hanlan snapped the TV off and set the remote on the coffee table. He straightened the file before he stood and stretched. "I'm going to bed."

Canin frowned, but before he could say anything his cell rang. He took it out and answered it with "Canin."

While Canin was occupied with the phone, Hanlan headed for the bathroom. If the call was important Canin would tell him. He started stripping his shirt off the second he hit the bathroom door, then tossed it into the hamper before he took a pit stop. The mirror showed he needed a shave, but he decided to do it in the morning, so he walked into the bedroom. Flipping on the bedside lamp, he sat down on the bed, then carefully took off his pants. Leaving them on the floor by the bed, he set his alarm before turning off the bedside lamp. He slid under the covers and moved onto his side, tucking himself in.

Though he had the heat on, the nights were cool. Winter was not far away and though the days were unseasonably warm, the nights showed the true season.

The bed moved as Canin jumped up and settled at his back.

When the Ruv slept with him his nightmares stayed away. With what he had seen today he needed the physical and mental warmth the Ruv gave him. And he had never liked to sleep alone. The closeness of another body satisfied something deep inside.

Canin gave a purr like rumble and Hanlan felt his weariness sweep over him, dragging him down into the depths of sleep.

CHAPTER 5

Hanlan awoke to find himself the little spoon to Canin. The Ruv had obviously transformed back to his human form while he slept. Which happened occasionally as the human form was their default. Self-preservation acted in weird ways sometimes.

Canin was wearing boxers and nothing else so he must have stripped last night before becoming the wolf. The Ruv was still on top of the covers but was wrapped around him like an octopus. How he had done that Hanlan didn't know.

His partner must have felt him awaken because he ran his nose along Hanlan's neck, sniffing.

The sensation caused a shiver to go up Hanlan's spine and warmth settled in his chest. There was nothing sexual about Canin's action. It was an instinct to insure that Hanlan was okay. Part of the companion—Shavora—deal. But it was hard to suppress years of human conditioning about male-to-male contact. Hanlan still tensed up sometimes, well, a lot.

His partner was obviously satisfied because he unwound himself from around Hanlan and rolled off the bed. He headed toward the bathroom, seemingly unconcerned about anything, as Hanlan threw back his covers.

Hanlan sat up on the edge of the bed, then hit his alarm before it could go off. He'd been waking up without it for years, but he knew that the one time he didn't set it would be the one time he wouldn't wake on time. That was just his luck. The toilet flushed and he stood up, stretching.

Canin came out of the bathroom wearing a pair of linen pants and a spun shirt. They shimmered and he was suddenly wearing a thin dark suit.

"That is so unfair," Hanlan told him. His partner just smiled at him as Hanlan headed for the bathroom himself. He forewent the shower, but he used his electric razor to shave. Usually he used a regular razor, but he didn't feel like it today. Back in the now empty bedroom he went to his closet and pulled out an older suit. He slipped it on, then grabbed his gun, wallets, and flip phone from last night's pants and settled them in their places in his new suit. After rolling up the old pants, he took them and dropped them in the bathroom's hamper.

"Breakfast is ready," Came Canin's voice through the door. He had seemingly went to the kitchen after Hanlan had gone into the bathroom that first time.

Hanlan exited the bathroom and headed for the kitchen. A plate of microwaved pancakes was set at his usual place and Canin was eating a waffle. Hanlan raised an eyebrow but sat down and started to eat.

"That was Phuro last night. He wanted to reiterate that Ms. Rose is not a member of his Pack and to thank us for bringing her to his attention as he had not known of her."

Hanlan paused in his eating. "I thought non-pack Ruv had to have the permission of the Alpha to reside in their territory."

"We do."

Canin's tone and feeling told Hanlan the subject was closed for now, so he resumed eating, finishing quickly. He grabbed both his own plate and Canin's and put them in the dishwasher before pouring himself and Canin a travel mug of coffee.

"Thanks," Canin said as he came to grab his mug.

Hanlan turned off the coffee maker, then headed for the back door. He grabbed his trench coat and threw it over his arm as he waited for Canin to join him. The Ruv always made a last round of the apartment when they left in the morning. Hanlan didn't ask him why. Some sort of Ruv instinct no doubt.

Canin came up beside him and flipped the outside light on. It was getting darker earlier and sometimes when they came home the sun was gone. Canin could see fine in the semi-dark, but Hanlan's human eyes saw only shadows.

The two of them exited the apartment and Hanlan locked the door before they headed to the car. Hanlan threw his coat in between the front seats, then slid in behind the wheel while Canin got in the passenger side. They drove to the station in silence. The two detectives came in as usual through the back of the station to miss the chaos of the front desk and took the back elevator up. When they got to the bullpen, they headed straight to their desks.

Hanlan slid into his chair and grabbed the phone. He dialed a number and put the headpiece to his ear. After a moment, he spoke. "Doctor Brennon. Glad I caught you in your office. Have you done the autopsies yet?" A pause. "Okay. Were there any defensive marks?" Another pause. "I see. Could you run an extended tox panel on both?" A longer pause. "Good. Thank you." He hung up the phone and looked over at Canin. "She had already ordered the panel as she had been suspicious after finding no defensive wounds."

"She's an excellent M. E."

"That she is." He scooted up to his computer and pulled up the form he needed. "I'm starting on the subpoena."

Canin took that as a hint and grabbed his desk phone.

While Canin was busy on the phone, Hanlan typed out the request, keeping to the bare facts. That was why judges loved his forms. No inculpatory statements or raw opinions, just facts.

Howell and Deneque came up to Hanlan's desk

as he finished the form.

"Morning, Gentlemen."

Canin had started on the notes, but he paused and looked at the two other detectives when Hanlan leaned back in his chair to greet them.

"I've got another subpoena for you two to serve at Barrington's," Hanlan told them.

Howell made a face.

"What did you find out about the other auction houses?" Hanlan asked, ignoring Howell's sourness. "Did he have any problems at any of them?"

"They stated that he was a respectable client in good standing. None of them reported any problems with other clients though he won quite often when he bid."

"None of the auction houses gave you any trouble with confidentiality?"

"No." Howell shook his head.

Hanlan threw a glance over to Canin, meeting his eyes for a second before turning his attention back to the other two detectives. "Grab the form and take it to Judge Peterson, then serve it."

"Meet back here after lunch?" Howell asked as he turned toward the front of the bullpen.

"We've got a meeting with Ms. Lupo at 1 pm." Canin inserted before Hanlan could say anything.

Howell turned back and raised an eyebrow. "Oh?"

"She was at the auction," Hanlan told him.

"Well, well, well." Howell shook his head, then he and Deneque headed to the printer by the front doors.

Canin turned back to his computer and started

typing again.

"Are you almost done?" Hanlan asked him.

"Just about. Why?"

"Thought we might drive by Kezia James' and Kezia Stein's last knowns."

"What sounds even better is an early lunch, then do the visits on the way to the Lupo Medical offices."

Hanlan raised an eyebrow when Canin glanced at him.

"She only agreed to meet there."

"Her territory."

Canin nodded, then scooted back from his computer. "All done."

"Let's get out of here before the Captain gets it in her mind to want an update." Hanlan stood and pushed his chair in under his desk. "We can grab something at Joey's."

"Sounds good." Canin got up and scooted his chair in.

They hurried out of there as if they were being pursued.

CHAPTER 6

The townhouse styled apartment building looked abandoned. There were boards covering broken windows and graffiti everywhere. A big padlock was on the front door.

Sitting on the front steps was an old woman. She was dressed in rags, but neat rags, with a shawl thrown over her shoulders. Her hair was done up in a bun and hoop earrings hung from her ears. A grocery cart covered by a blanket set at the bottom of the stairs.

"She might know something," Canin told Hanlan.

Hanlan nodded and both of them got out of the car. They approached the woman slowly with their hands visible and stopped by her cart.

"Is this 528 Mercer Street?" Hanlan asked her.

"Yes." She eyed them for a moment, then asked, "You looking for Kezia?"

"Why would you ask that?" Hanlan raised an eyebrow.

"That girl is trouble with a capital T."

"Oh?"

The old woman nodded but didn't elaborate.

"Do you know where she went?"

"She left before we were evicted. Been gone for two months now. She moved in with her boyfriend."

"Do you know his name?"

"Davidson, I think. She always called him Randy. I only met him once."

"Thank you." Canin handed her a folded-up bill. "You've been very helpful."

"Will you be okay?" Hanlan asked her.

The old woman held her hand around the bill tightly as she nodded.

Both detectives turned and walked back to the car. They slid into the vehicle and Hanlan drove off.

Their lunch had been leisurely. Neither of them had been in a big hurry to get back to work, but they had known it needed to be done. Kezia James' place had been closest so that had been where they had headed when they had finally aroused themselves.

"Randy Davidson. Why is that name familiar?" Hanlan wondered aloud. "I know I know that name from somewhere."

"You'll think of it. We got time to check out Stein's place?"

"Yeah." He paused. "I hate situations like that.

Old people not having any place to go."

"I gave her Nodi's card with that bill."

Nodi was a Ruv healer who ran a homeless shelter in the city. Hanlan had met her a couple of weeks ago when he had gotten shot. He had encountered her a few more times since.

"Hopefully she'll use it."

They drove in silence for a few more minutes, then Hanlan turned into another residential street. There were some single-family homes but most of the older houses on this street looked to be converted into apartments. He found a parking place, then they got out of the car and headed toward the second house behind their spot.

Their quarry was coming out the front door as the detectives stepped onto the porch. They all stopped and stared at each other for a moment. Her short hair was cut in a pixie style and her green eyes were wary. A bit of change from her picture.

"Kezia Stein?" Hanlan asked.

"Who wants to know?" Her voice was carefully neutral.

"I'm Detective Hanlan and this is my partner Detective Canin. We'd like to ask you a few questions."

"What's this about?" Again her voice was neutral.

"We just need to know where you were Monday afternoon until early Tuesday morning."

"Don't you guys talk to each other?" she asked.

Hanlan just raised an eyebrow.

"I was in jail. Just released this morning."

"Ah. Thank you for your time, Ms. Stein."

Hanlan gave her a nod, then both detectives turned and went back down the stairs.

"She must have still been being processed when we ran the check," Canin said as they headed toward their car.

"We'll see when we get back."

When they got to the car, they slid inside, then Hanlan pulled out and drove away. It was a little early, but Hanlan was sure Lupo wouldn't mind. She'd want this to be over with as soon as possible, just as he did.

Ten minutes later, Hanlan pulled up to the guard booth and gate of the Lupo Medical offices. The square office building was set back about a hundred yards from the street and was blocked off with a wrought iron fence. Behind the office building was the labs themselves.

The female guard stepped out of the booth with a clipboard and moved to the driver's window which Hanlan slid down. "May I help you?"

"Detectives Hanlan and Canin to see Ms. Julia Lupo." Hanlan flipped out his badge wallet and Canin showed his. "We have an appointment."

The guard ran her finger down the clipboard, stopping half-way down, then nodded. "You're authorized to enter. You'll be met in the lobby," she told them before moving back to the guard booth.

Seconds later the gate opened, and Hanlan drove inside, slipping his badge into his jacket pocket. He parked as close to the front door as possible, then they both exited the car.

They headed toward the glass front door. The building was all steel and glass, making it look modern although it was over thirty years old. They entered and stopped just inside.

The two-story lobby was expansive and bright with all the windows. A large desk sat in the middle with a guard and monitors. Behind the desk was a set of elevators and to the left and right were glass and steel stairs, leading to a walkway and the upper floor. Plants dotted the area, relieving the sterileness of the lobby.

A blond woman came down the stairs on the right and stopped half-way between the detectives and the stairway. "Detectives."

Her voice carried to them, and they moved towards her. She looked like a pixie, small and delicate looking, but Hanlan was sure she had a strong personality. Working for Lupo could not be easy.

"I am Jessica Croft, Ms. Lupo's PA," she told them as soon as they stopped in front of her. "I'm here to take you to her office."

"Alright." Hanlan noted she was not Ruv which surprised him a bit. He had figured Lupo would surround herself with her own.

Croft turned and headed back to the stairs with them following after her. She led the way up the stairs and down the main hallway to the end office.

The outer area held two desks, one of which was occupied, and a waiting area with a refreshment table. But Croft led them to the door in the back wall and opened it to usher them in.

Julia Lupo was standing behind her fancy wooden desk, staring out the large picture window that took up almost the whole wall. Bookshelves lined the other walls and two wood chairs sat before the desk. There was a large rug that covered half the room instead of carpeting. It looked more like a den rather than an office of a multi-million-dollar business.

Hanlan and Canin moved to the desk and Lupo turned her head to watch them while Croft closed the door, leaving the two of them alone with Lupo. The three of them stared at each other for a moment before Lupo moved and sat at her desk with a gesture to the chairs.

When they were all settled, Lupo spoke. "I didn't really know Mr. Ruthridge as I don't use his company. However I have seen him several times at auctions."

"According to Barrington's list, you were at the auction Monday night," Hanlan told her.

"Yes, I was there. I bought some very nice books to add to my library."

"You do know that the proceeds from that auction went to the Trust?"

"I go to all of the Trust Charity Auctions," Lupo told him. "I find it amusing that they use my money for their work,"

"They probably do too," Hanlan returned. "Did you know that books from the Graves' estate were being auctioned that night?"

"Of course. It was in the sale brochure I got." She opened the right-hand upper drawer of the desk and pulled out a magazine. Closing the drawer, she tossed the magazine to Canin before putting her elbows on the desktop and resting her head on her hands.

"We were told Ruthridge had a spirited bidding war with a woman for those books."

"Ah. Sorry to disappoint you, Detective, but it wasn't me."

"Then who was it?" he asked her.

"I don't know. She definitely wasn't a regular. As I said I attend every Trust Charity Auction and quite a few of Barrington's regular auctions. I never saw her at any of them."

"Can you describe her?"

"About thirty with long dark hair, dark eyes, pale coloring. You humans would probably find her quite attractive."

"Was she with anyone?" Hanlan asked, ignoring the sideways dig.

"Not that I saw. An usher escorted her from the room after Ruthridge won the bid. She got quite disruptive."

"I'm sure. Where did you go after the auction?"

"Here to drop off the books, then for a run."

"A run as in..." He left it hanging for her to answer.

"Wolf time, yes."

"So no alibi."

Lupo just stared at him.

Hanlan stood and Canin followed him a moment later. "That's all I have right now, but I'm sure I'll be talking to you again."

"If it's about this, you can just talk to my attorney. This was a courtesy to your partner."

Hanlan ignored this dig as well. He turned and headed for the door with Canin just behind him. When he opened the door he found Croft waiting for them.

She led them back out of the office and down the hallway to the stairs. "I'll let you go the rest of the way yourselves, Detectives."

They could feel both her eyes and the guard's eyes on them until the front door closed behind them. The detectives went to the car and got in.

"Can we believe her?" Hanlan asked. "About anything she said?"

"I don't know." Canin was frowning.

Hanlan made a face, then drove toward the gate. He waved to the guard as she let them out, then headed back to the station. Howell and Deneque would be back by now and they should have started on the background checks on Barrington's employees. Perhaps they would get another lead.

CHAPTER 7

Howell and Deneque were indeed back and working on background checks. Hanlan and Canin took a copy of the list to their desks and started at the bottom, working their way up. They worked silently but for the click-clack of their typing.

Hanlan surfaced when someone cleared their throat nearby. He looked and saw the captain standing beside his desk. "Captain."

"The mayor called me for an update. I told him we have leads we're pursuing. Tell me I wasn't lying."

"You're not." Hanlan told her about the woman bidder and the old case which both had Barrington's in common. "We're going through the employees right now."

"And the bidder?"

"We have a list." He paused for a second, then said, "Ms. Julia Lupo was one of bidders. We spoke to her briefly after lunch and she denied being the hostile bidder. But she doesn't have a verifiable alibi."

"Second time she's come up regarding a homicide." The captain frowned. "She's either very busy or very unlucky."

Hanlan gave her a grim smile at the attempted humor.

"Keep me apprised." She turned on her heels and headed back to her office from which a faint ringing could be heard.

Hanlan looked over at Canin who was frowning at his computer screen. "Find something?"

"Howell sent over a name. Nick James."

"Any relation to Kezia James?"

"According to this he's her brother. He bailed her out last time she was arrested. And he's got a sealed juvie record. That's what caught Howell's eye."

"We don't have enough probable cause for a judge to unseal it yet. No recent violations?"

"No." Canin shook his head.

"Do you know what he does at Barrington's?"

"No."

"We'll have to send the boys back or visit ourselves then." Hanlan tapped his desk thoughtfully. "Anything else come up?"

"Nothing in my bunch. Yours?"

"Seems Ms. Stein works at Barrington's."

Canin raised an eyebrow. "You think she's

running a con?"

Hanlan shrugged. "Don't know. However she was in jail. Midnight Monday until this morning."

"So until we have TOD we can't rule her out."

"Brennon should send us a preliminary tonight, so we'll have it tomorrow when we come in. The tox panel will be a few days. Maybe longer since tomorrow's Thanksgiving."

Howell and Deneque stopped beside Hanlan's desk. "Do you need us to come in tomorrow?" Howell asked when Canin and Hanlan looked at them.

"Need an excuse to get away from the in-laws?" Hanlan asked back.

Deneque smiled as his partner groaned an affirmative "Yes."

"You should have volunteered for the shift then," Hanlan told him unsympathetically.

"You already had," Howell said.

Hanlan shrugged. He and Canin both didn't have any family or plans so they had volunteered when the notice went up. Neither of them were sentimental either so they probably would be working Christmas too. Losing family whether through death or divorce didn't engender good feelings around the holidays.

"We finished our list and besides that one I sent Canin, didn't find anything suspicious."

Picking up a piece of paper off his desk, Hanlan handed it to Howell. "You can check out those three woman."

"The female bidder?" Howell asked as he took the paper.

"Yeah. Canin and I are looking up the other two. One of which was indeed our old friend Julia Lupo by the way."

"And how was your interview?"

"Nominal."

Howell nodded, then straightened up a bit. "Well, I'll put this on my desk, but Deneque and I thought we'd get out of here a little early."

Hanlan glanced at the clock and saw that it was an hour until shift was over. "Then get. We'll see you Friday."

Both detectives nodded and headed back toward their desks.

"Hopefully, we don't get busy tomorrow." Canin leaned back and stretched. "We already have two other cases on hold because of this one."

"And the rest of the paperwork for the one we closed Monday," Hanlan agreed. "Though the Larson Case was getting cold."

Before Canin could say anything his cell phone beeped that he had a text. He took it out of his pocket and looked at it, hitting some buttons with his thumb. A frown crossed his face.

"What is it?"

"Phuro wants to see us after work."

"Did he say why?"

"No." Canin slipped his phone back in his pocket. "He just says to meet him at the library."

"Will you do the notes?"

Canin nodded and started working on his computer.

Hanlan straightened up his desk, keeping his eye out for the night desk officer. One of Brennon's assistants would have dropped off her preliminary report at the front desk on their way home by now, and the officer would bring it up during one of his breaks or have one of the uniforms do so. Hanlan really wanted to look at it before he and Canin left for their meeting with Phuro.

However, neither the desk officer nor a uniform showed by the time Canin scooted away from his computer ten minutes later. Both detectives stood and pushed their chairs in, then headed for the front doors. The bullpen was nearly deserted except for the two swing shift pairs.

Day shift was from 7 a.m. to 5 p.m., but swing and night shifts were marginally shorter. Swing was from 3 p.m. to 11 p.m. and consisted of two detective pairs while night went from 10:30 p.m. to 7:30 a.m. and consisted of one detective pair. If needed a day shift pair was called in during another shift. During Thanksgiving and Christmas usually only one pair was on duty during the day unless they had need of another pair. The rest of the shifts ran as usual.

The detectives rode the elevator down in silence. Reach was not at his desk,, so they continued on outside. Once at the car, they got in and Hanlan drove out into the evening traffic which was heavier than usual due to the holiday tomorrow.

It took Hanlan a little longer to get to the library but since they didn't have a set time to be there he was sure Phuro wouldn't mind. He drove around back and pulled up next to a new-looking VW Bug parked at the fence.

The detectives got out of the car and headed

down the ramp to the door at the bottom. Hanlan rapped on it when they got there, and it opened almost immediately to reveal an impatient-looking Phuro.

"About time," Phuro muttered as he hurried them inside before re-locking the door. Hanlan merely raised an eyebrow and Phuro looked sheepish. "Sorry. But it's important." He led them into the library where the detectives were surprised to see Jami Rose standing by the special display case.

She gave Hanlan a nod, then looked at Phuro who stared back.

"Will one of you please explain," Hanlan said into the silence.

"She's an Oru," Phuro told him rather bluntly.

Hanlan raised an eyebrow.

Rose looked amused. "He ran a test," she told Hanlan. "The full results are pending, but preliminary results confirm."

"Okay." He drew out the word sort of questioningly. *Why were they here* clear in his tone.

"I asked him to have you come." Rose turned to face them more fully. "The Trust aren't the only— hunters in the City."

"The rogue pikie," Phuro said. His voice was dismissive.

"Only they're not rogue anymore," Rose told him. "Over the centuries they formed a loose band of their own. They call themselves the Kal'endral or simply the Kal. Their hatred and rhetoric have been passed through the generations."

Phuro made a dismissive gesture, but Hanlan raised an eyebrow. "You think one of them killed

Ruthridge."

"Yes. They have been hunting the Lexicon themselves. I think the Kal had finally caught on to Raven Manor's secret. And had the Graves' been still alive, they would have been the victims."

"Do you think they know about the Trust?" Canin asked.

"I don't know. But I wouldn't put it past them."

Phuro was frowning. "You believe this Kal is responsible for the murders Hanlan is investigating."

It wasn't a question, but Rose nodded. "Yes."

"And that they are after the Lexicon."

Again she nodded. "Yes."

"The Book had been a nearly forgotten legend by the time we were with the Chosen."

"Far from forgotten by the Loupe," she disagreed. "They used to tell of how the Oru had kept the Book from them, the 'rightful heirs'."

Hanlan heard something in her tone, and Phuro must have too as the elder looked at her sharply. However, the female Ruv's face remained serene.

"So you think this Kal is acting on misinformation?" Hanlan asked her.

"Yes."

"This will fit into our Occult angle we were using," Canin said.

"Which reminds me. Did you find out what those symbols mean?" Hanlan asked Phuro.

The Ruv elder just stared at him silently.

"What symbols?" Rose asked.

"There was similar murders in 1989. Two symbols were drawn on the wall."

"Can I see them?" she asked, taking a step toward them.

"That won't be necessary," Phuro said, taking a step forward himself.

Rose silenced the rest of his words with a look and moved to stand near the detectives. "Please."

Canin got out his phone and showed her the picture of the symbols.

She shot Phuro another look before addressing the two detectives. "Those symbols stand for The Beginning and The End. They represent a prophecy of the fate of the World."

"I gather it's not good since Phuro doesn't want to bring it up."

"It's been misinterpreted by many, including the Kal." Her glance at Phuro told Hanlan that she included the Ruv elder in that misinterpretation bit.

Phuro opened his mouth, but Hanlan spoke first. "So this prophecy is why this Kal is after the Lexicon?"

"Yes. They think it will bring about the end of the Ruv. The Hunters think it will mean the Ruv will rule over humans. And a lot of the Ruv elders believe variants of both."

"I gather none of that is true?"

"It's all in the interpretation of the wording. Or should I say misinterpretation."

"We have the original wording..." Phuro began.

"The original interpretation, you mean," Rose interrupted. "When it was first translated, the Ruv who read it gave her interpretation of what she thought it said."

Phuro inclined his head in acknowledgment of

her point.

"Can someone tell me what this prophecy is because I have no idea what you all are talking about." Hanlan looked back and forth between Phuro and Rose. "And it might help us stop the killer."

The Ruv elder frowned and started to shake his head, but Rose shot him a look and he subsided.

Hanlan tilted his head and looked at Rose with a raised eyebrow.

"A Shavora should be respected," she told him in answer. "A lot of things have been forgotten or dismissed, but that should—and must not be. Shavora are our salvation."

Hanlan raised the other eyebrow.

But before Rose could say anything else they heard raised voices from the archway leading to the librarian's desk. They all turned to see Gayl enter with three men. She was trying to stop them, but they kept pushing past her.

One of the men was Bryan Deneque.

CHAPTER 8

“It is alright, Ms. Gayl,” Phuro said. “They are here for me.”

“This is most irregular, Professor.” She spoke in a stern voice.

“And I apologize.”

She gave a huff and went back through the archway while the three men came closer. The two men with Deneque were obviously bully boys, two of his Hunters no doubt.

“What is happening here, Professor Ulven?” Deneque was looking at Rose as he spoke.

“We asked the Professor to look at some books for us, but he told us he was not a specialist in that field, so he said he'd find us one.” Hanlan spoke up to draw Deneque's attention away from Rose.

"When they explained what they wanted, I told them I had already looked at those books for you, but I would gladly look to see if any were missing," Rose continued smoothly. "We were about to set a time for that when you came in."

Deneque stared into her eyes for a moment, then looked at Phuro. "That's why they were here the other day?"

Phuro nodded.

"We added him as an unpaid consultant," Hanlan told Deneque. "It's useful to have someone with his credentials helping us."

"I'm sure it is." He seemed to relax a bit. "Professor Simpson was a bit concerned about you," he told Phuro.

"I'm fine. Just distracted a bit. My work will not suffer."

"See that it doesn't." Deneque glanced at the two detectives, then turned and walked away with his two men at his heels.

They watched him leave through the archway, then waited until Gayl appeared in the arch herself.

"I'm sorry, Phuro." She bowed her head.

"Not your fault. You can go back to your work."

She bowed her head again, then went back through the archway.

"He wasn't here to check up on you the way he made it sound," Hanlan said. "He wasn't worried about you."

"No." Phuro shook his head. "I'm a stalking horse."

"The question is whether he had you followed or is he staking this library out."

"I'll be finding that out." Phuro promised. "I've been cautious but then Hunters are good at stalking us."

"Let's set a time to meet at Ruthridge's on Friday and I'll speak with you then," Rose told Hanlan. "Mr. Deneque no doubt left someone to watch and if we stay for long he will get even more suspicious."

"What about your boss, Mr. Barrington?" Hanlan asked her. "I get the feeling he and Deneque are tight."

"I took the day off. What I do on my time is my business."

"Let's hope he agrees with that." Hanlan paused. "Is 9 a.m., good?"

"Perfect." She and Phuro headed toward the back door.

"You alright?" Hanlan asked Canin. "You were awfully quiet."

"She was giving off Alpha smell/vibes."

Hanlan raised an eyebrow.

"We have respect for females anyway but with the Alpha smell, I was a bit..."

"Intimidated?" Hanlan asked when Canin broke off.

"Something like that."

Phuro came back and joined them. "Did you need to speak to me, Detective?"

"I just want to ensure that the Lexicon is safe. If the Hunters break in..." He didn't need to continue that thought he was sure.

"Here it's just another book in the collection. They won't suspect anything different just by looking."

Hanlan spared a glance at the case, then turned on his heel and headed for the back door with Canin just behind him. The Book was no longer his responsibility so he shouldn't worry. But concern nagged at him anyway.

Phuro hurried past them and unlocked the outer door for them. Once they were outside, they heard him lock it and they went up the ramp. It was dark but the building lights lit the area well enough for them to see. The VW Bug was gone so Hanlan figured it must have been Rose's. After a glance around the detectives headed toward their car and got in as soon as they reached it.

Neither detective spoke on the drive home.

Hanlan had told Canin all the stories his great grandmother had told him about the Ruv when he was a boy, but he realized Canin hadn't told him any of the Ruv legends that he had been taught growing up. Canin always managed to distract him when Hanlan asked about them. Hanlan knew Canin had had a rough childhood and the circumstances surrounding the death of Canin's 'family' and suspected that that was the root of his evasiveness. Much like his ex-wife was the root of a lot of his own baggage.

He pulled into his parking slot at his apartment, then grabbed Canin's arm when he moved to open his door. "Wait."

Canin froze and, seeing where Hanlan was staring, looked as well.

The entryway to their apartment was dark.

Light from the homeowners' back door didn't

reach down there though the light was on as it was every night. Which was why they always turned on their own light before they left in the morning.

Hanlan flipped the headlights back on, illuminating the top part of the seemingly empty entryway. They both got out carefully and Hanlan slipped his hand behind his back to rest on his gun as they moved forward cautiously. Nothing jumped out at them and Hanlan relaxed when the entryway proved truly empty.

Canin flickered a gaze at his hand and a green ball of light formed between his fingers. The glow lit the area before the door, revealing broken glass from the overhead light and the gift left for them.

A knife pinned a tarot card and what looked like a human heart to a small square wooden board leaning against their door. The board was soaked with blood, but the concrete and door was not so Hanlan knew it had been created elsewhere and brought here. However, blood was dripping down which meant it had been done recently.

One-handedly Canin took out his phone and snapped pictures of it before hitting a button and putting the phone to his ear. "Howell, this is Detective Canin, I need a CSU at mine and Detective Hanlan's apartment," he said a few seconds later into it. "It seems we were left a present from the Ruthridges' killer." He paused. "Okay. See you in a few minutes." Canin returned his phone to his pocket. "He'll be here in ten. You'd best get your flashlight and turn off the headlights before he gets here."

Hanlan nodded and returned to the car. He

reached under the seat for his mag light, then switched off the headlights before heading back to the entryway.

Canin extinguished his ball of light and Hanlan flipped on his flashlight. They both stood at the foot of the stairs while Hanlan kept his light on the 'gift'.

"How did the killer know we were the detectives on the case? Unless it is indeed Lupo."

"Barrington knows as well," Canin said. "And Deneque, though the timing would be tight for him."

"Their feet are too big to be the killer," Hanlan dismissed.

"Accomplices? Instigators?"

Headlights hit them and Canin ran up the stairs while Hanlan remained where he was. Moments later Canin and Howell descended the stairway and joined him at the bottom. It was a tight fit for two so Canin stayed on the last step.

"I see you got an admirer, Hanlan," Howell said, nodding toward the 'gift'.

"So it would seem." Hanlan kept his thoughts to himself. He and Canin would discuss this later when they had privacy. In the meantime he would just go with the flow and act clueless. "We must have gotten close somewhere to trigger this response."

Another set of headlights hit them and Canin went back up the stairs to meet what should be the CSU techs.

"Want me to call the Captain?" Howell asked Hanlan.

"If you would."

"Not a problem."

Hanlan and Howell moved aside as much as they could as the CSU tech came down the stairs. She stopped on the bottom step and glanced around, then set down her case before running back up the stairs. Moments later she appeared with a battery-powered lamp.

"I'll get out of your way," Hanlan told her as he mounted the stairway. Howell followed him up to the top where Canin was waiting.

"I'd tell you to go home, but..." Howell said with a grin.

"I should probably check my front door as well," Hanlan told him.

"Front door?"

"Yep." Hanlan flashed him a smile. "This apartment comes with two doors."

"Let's look then."

The three detectives walked around the side of the house on the gravel walkway, Hanlan's flashlight lighting the way. Hanlan opened the small wrought iron gate that blocked the lower stairway and led the way down to the covered front entryway. It was empty of any 'gifts'.

"Go on inside," Howell said. He pulled out a small mag light from his coat pocket and turned it on. "I'll take care of the scene."

"Sorry to disturb you tonight."

"I should be thanking you. My in-laws were there when I got home."

"I thought they weren't supposed to be there 'til tomorrow morning."

"Neither did I."

His aggravated tone made Hanlan laugh. Howell and his father-in-law disliked each other immensely. The less time they spent together the better. "Maybe they'll be asleep when you return."

"I can only hope."

Hanlan got out his keys and opened the front door he rarely used with a hard push. He and Canin went inside and locked the door behind them. Glancing around the little foyer, he didn't see anything disturbed. The table by the door was the only furnishing and it was in its place. He picked up the magazine and two envelopes from the floor and laid them on the table. They weren't bills so he would look at them later.

The two of them continued on into the living area with Canin heading for the kitchen while Hanlan headed into the bathroom. Hanlan made a pit stop, then went back out into the living room and dropped onto the sofa.

Canin came out of the kitchen with two beers and handed one to his partner.

Hanlan took a long drink, then looked at Canin who was still standing there. "We need to talk about this, but I really just want to forget about it."

Canin sat his beer on the coffee table and with a shimmer took on his wolf form. He jumped on the sofa and laid down with his head on his partner's lap.

Hanlan started to pet Canin and took periodic sips of his beer. They stayed like that for about an hour before Hanlan began to talk. He went back through what they knew but nothing special stood out to him. At least nothing to him to warrant such a response from the killer.

Ruthridge and his wife had been killed Monday night by person or persons unknown after attending an auction at Barrington's. He had an argument at said auction with a female bidder over his winning the lot they were both bidding on. Hanlan and Canin had gotten both employee records and the attendance list from Barrington's and were going through them. Nothing seems out of place at Ruthridge's work according to Howell and Deneque. So far the mundane leads were—mundane.

Shifting a bit, Canin shimmered and returned to his human form. He pulled out his phone and called up the pictures he had taken of the 'gift'.

"That still gets to me," Hanlan said. "Those energy pockets that you say you stash things in, they would have to be inside you if I reckon right."

"I'm sending Phuro the pics." Canin tapped the phone, seeming to ignore Hanlan's words. "The Tarot is the Death Card, but it doesn't literally mean death, just change."

"I'm pretty sure the killer meant it literally." Hanlan allowed the change of subject. He was tired. In more ways than one. "I just hope that heart came from one of the Ruthridges and we don't have another murder out there."

Canin sat up and slipped his phone back in its pocket before standing and offering his hand to Hanlan. "Come on. Let's go to bed."

Hanlan barked out a laugh but took Canin's hand and allowed his partner to pull him to his feet.

CHAPTER 9

When he awoke, Hanlan found himself in an increasingly familiar position; the little spoon to Canin's big one. The Ruv must be becoming more comfortable with Hanlan's proximity. While the human form was their default when the Ruv sleep they usually stayed in the form they started with, especially if in wolf form.

Canin ran his nose along Hanlan's neck from the back of the ear to the hollow of his shoulder and a pleasant shiver went up Hanlan's spine.

The Shavora bond was intimate, but not necessarily sexual. After what his ex-wife put him through he had not been interested in a relationship. He had missed the intimacy, the closeness of another body, but not the sex per se. With this bond he got what he needed right now without messy complications.

"You smell strongly of yourself," Canin murmured

"Is that your way of saying I need a shower?"

Canin huffed a laugh, his breath on Hanlan's neck causing the human to shiver, before he untangled himself from Hanlan and flopped back on the bed.

Hanlan threw back the bedding, covering part of Canin's body, and sat up on the edge of the bed. "You didn't answer me."

"I like the way you smell."

"That's still not an answer." Hanlan stood and made his way to the bathroom, grabbing a pair of boxers on the way. Once inside he stripped and stepped inside the shower. He turned the water on and quickly washed, using his partner's expensive soap and shampoo. After he rinsed, he turned the water off, then grabbed a towel as he stepped out of the shower. He thoroughly dried himself before he slipped on the fresh boxers and tossed his pajama bottoms and towel in the hamper. A pit stop at the toilet, then he turned toward the door to his bedroom.

Canin came in and stopped, sniffing. He stepped closer and took a deep breath. Pleasure lit his eyes and flooded the bond. "Now you smell like me."

That had been the plan. Hanlan knew Canin liked it better when he could smell himself or his products on Hanlan. It was sort of a payback for that crack about him smelling more like himself. To Hanlan that meant he stunk, no matter what it meant to Canin.

Hanlan slipped by his partner and headed into the bedroom. He grabbed a newer suit from his closet and put it—and his other stuff--on before going out to the living room. Canin passed him on his way to the kitchen, wearing a thin dark suit. The cold never bothered Canin.

By the time Hanlan made it to the kitchen, Canin had two breakfast burritos done and two coffees set on the table. Both of them ate while standing and put the rest of the coffee in travel mugs when they finished. Canin reset the coffee maker, then did his rounds while Hanlan retrieved his flashlight and went to wait by the back door.

When Canin joined him, Hanlan opened the door and glanced around. No crime scene tape greeted them, and Hanlan let out a relieved breath before stepping outside. Not even the blood remained. The CSU techs must have cleaned it before they left because he didn't think Howell would have done it. They weren't that close, and CSU liked Hanlan. He didn't get in their way or had too many requests for them outside their bivouac.

After Hanlan secured the door, both detectives headed for the car. A folded sheet of paper was stuck under the driver side windshield wiper. Canin snapped a picture before Hanlan pulled the paper from the wiper and opened it, causing a tied string to fall out. He caught it before it fell all the way to the ground and held it as he read the two words on the paper.

"Well?" Canin asked in the continued silence.

"Mulengi Dori."

"Dead man's string," his partner translated. "Someone is calling on the spirits to protect you."

Hanlan returned the string to the paper, then folded it smaller before slipping it into his inner jacket pocket. "We need to get going."

Canin nodded, then both of them got into the car. They remained silent for the twenty-minute drive. Once at the station Hanlan parked in his usual place, then they both got out of the car and ran up the stairs. The back lobby was empty, so they continued on straight for the elevator and rode it up to the fourth floor. An empty bullpen greeted them when they arrived, and they headed immediately for their desks.

"Looks like we got the preliminary autopsy report." Hanlan sat down and reached into his inbox to pull out a file envelope. He opened the envelope and pulled out the report. The envelope was tossed on his desk, then he flipped through the document.

Canin sat down at his own desk and waited.

"Both hearts are accounted for," Hanlan told him, still looking through the report.

"So we got another body somewhere."

"Yes." Before he could say more his phone rang. He laid the report on the desk, then answered with the customary "Hanlan." There was a pause, then, "Where?" Another pause. "Alright. Thank you." He hung up the phone and stood. "That was dispatch. Body in an alley."

"So much for a quiet day." Canin stood as well. "Any particulars?"

"No."

The detectives strode out of the bullpen to the

elevator and rode down in silence. They hurried out to the car and got in. The drive took them a little over thirty minutes as there was little traffic, and the scene was near the edge of their area. Hanlan parked behind a patrol car that was blocking the back street and both detectives got out. They headed to the mouth of the alley where a uniform awaited them just outside the tape.

"Officer Johnson," Hanlan greeted the uniform.

"Detectives." Johnson nodded to them. "It's a bad one."

Hanlan raised an eyebrow.

"You'll see."

"Alright. You first on scene?" Hanlan asked him.

"Yeah. Dave and I were chasing a robbery suspect and he darted in here. He tried to hide the loot in a pile of garbage but found something already buried there. Froze him long enough for Dave to catch up and nab him." Johnson lifted up the tape for them to walk under. "CSU and the M.E. are waiting for you."

Hanlan and Canin slipped into the alley and headed for the area between the two dumpsters where the two CSU techs and Dr. Brennon were squatting. Dirt and faded graffiti covered the walls. Garbage littered the alley everywhere and the smell of rotting meat assaulted the two detectives the closer they got to the dumpsters.

Dr. Brennon saw them coming and stood while the tech kept working. "Hanlan, Canin."

"Doc." Hanlan returned as he and Canin stopped beside Dr. Brennon. He turned his head and stared at the mess between the dumpsters.

Trash surrounded the sprawled body of a naked young man. His chest cavity was split open, and the heart was obviously missing but there was no other signs of trauma visible.

"So what do you know?" Hanlan asked Brennon.

"Not much beside the obvious," she told him. "No ID of course. Though they haven't searched all the trash yet. Look, I heard about last night."

"You think the heart came from him?"

"It's a possibility. CSU will do his DNA, so I told them to run it against the heart."

Hanlan nodded but was looking at the body with a frown.

"Something wrong?" she asked him.

"He looks familiar."

"The Ruthridge crime scene," Canin told him. "He was the uniform at the front door."

"Randy Davidson." Hanlan snapped his fingers. "Kezia James' boyfriend. I knew I had seen that name somewhere. I should have recognized it sooner."

"His partner was the one who filled out the report. Davidson's name was only mentioned once," Canin told him. "You may have a phenomenal memory but you're only human."

"Still." Hanlan shook his head, then spoke in a loud voice to the two techs. "He's one of ours. A patrolman."

Both techs paused for a moment, then with a nod went back to gathering evidence.

Two morgue assistants arrived just then with a gurney and a body bag.

"I'll get the preliminary to you as soon as

possible. And run an extended tox screen on him" Brennon told them.

"Good." Hanlan took one last look, then he and Canin headed back toward the mouth. "We need to talk to Davidson's partner and search his place. But with the holiday we won't get a judge to sign off today."

"Perhaps a car to watch the place?"

"I'll see what I can do."

The two of them walked under the tape and went back to their car. They got in and Hanlan drove them back to the station. Canin called the Duty Sargent while they were driving so that by the time they arrived at the precinct Davidson's partner was waiting for them. He met them on the fourth floor, and they went into the small conference room.

Hanlan and Canin sat on one side of the table while the officer sat on the other.

"Is this about what happened at the Ruthridge scene?" the officer blurted out. "Randy's a rookie. He didn't mean to contaminate the scene."

"Officer O'Malley, I'm sorry to be the one to tell you this, but Davidson was found dead this morning in an alley." Hanlan didn't pull his punches. "By the condition of his body, he's been dead at least a day."

"No." O'Malley shook his head. "He's been home sick the last two days. I just talked to his girlfriend an hour ago."

"Kezia James?" Hanlan asked him as Canin suddenly got up and left.

"Don't know her last name, but yeah Kezia."

"Did you call her, or did she call you?"

"She wanted to keep me in the loop. We'd only

been partners for a few months, but Randy doesn't have any family."

Canin came back with a file. He opened it and showed the photo inside to O'Malley. "This her?"

"I only saw her twice, but yes that's her."

"Kezia James," Canin confirmed. "What's Davidson's address?"

"1234 Olander Street," O'Malley answered. "Apartment 2C."

"I'll send a unit," Canin said as he disappeared out the door.

"I just can't believe she'd have anything to do with this. She seemed such a nice girl."

"Part of her charm. Did you notice anything different about Davidson after the Ruthridge scene?"

"He seemed distracted, and he went home early that day. He told me he was not feeling well. I just figured it was the scene itself. Some people just can't handle it."

"I sent the unit." Canin stepped back in the room. "I also put a BOLO out on Kezia James. I have a feeling she's not going to be at the apartment."

"Does Davidson have a car?"

"No." O'Malley shook his head. "Motorcycle."

Canin left again.

"You'll keep me in the loop about Randy?"

"I'll tell you what I can when I can," Hanlan told him.

"Good enough." O'Malley got up. "I best get back."

Hanlan nodded, then watched the officer leave

before getting up himself. He was not feeling anything from O'Malley. The Training Officer didn't seem broken up or even really upset about his partner's death. But maybe O'Malley just wasn't the emotional type. Hanlan moved to the door, then joined his partner out in the hallway.

"I didn't get a lot of love from O'Malley," Canin said.

"He said they were only partners for a few months. Maybe he's not invested. Some Training Officers keep detached."

"The good ones don't."

"What do you say to an early lunch after we do the notes and preliminary report?" Hanlan asked.

"Sounds good to me."

"Then let's get to it."

Both detectives headed down the hall toward the bullpen. They had paperwork to do.

CHAPTER 10

Hanlan's desk phone rang just as the two detectives returned from lunch. They both sat down before Hanlan answered his phone with his customary "Hanlan." He paused, then spoke again. "Sorry your holiday was interrupted, Captain." Another pause, then "It won't interfere." A longer pause. "Thank you, Captain. See you tomorrow then." He hung up the phone.

"She just hear about last night?"

"Yeah. Howell left her a message when he couldn't reach her last night and she just heard it. She's coming in tomorrow to talk to us."

"She didn't have to interrupt her holiday vacation. She could have waited until Monday."

"She's thinking about pulling us. That 'gift' could

be for either one of us or both of us after all."

"So that's why she's coming in."

"Yeah." He had noticed an envelope in his inbox. It was black and larger than average. He carefully took it out and, after putting on gloves, opened it. A tarot card was inside, and he pulled it out very cautiously, causing a bit of dust to fall to his desk. He stopped breathing and scooted back, keeping the card over the desk. Thankfully he hadn't inhaled any of the dust. He turned the card over to see its face.

It was another death card.

"Well, we now know who it's for." Hanlan dropped the card to his desk.

Canin growled. He stood, then moved to Hanlan's side and pulled the human to his feet. Jerking his partner forward, Canin hugged Hanlan and buried his face into the human's neck.

"The cameras," Hanlan hissed, trying to pull away. He felt a flare of something from his partner before the Ruv allowed him to move back. "We need to call CSU," he said as he straightened his clothing.

His partner nodded and pulled out his cell.

While Canin made the call, Hanlan studied the powder that had come from the envelope. He was pretty sure it was LSD or something similar. Of course it could be anthrax just as well. He wasn't an expert on drugs by any means, but he hadn't felt any deadliness from the envelope, even with the death card. After all these years he had learned to trust his 'feelings'.

"They said they'd be up in a few minutes. I also

called Howell. He said he'd be here in thirty."

"Guess I should call the Captain."

"Let Howell do that." Canin shook his head.

His partner was standing in his personal space, hovering, but Hanlan didn't say anything. If it made Canin feel better, he'd let him hover. But that hug could get them a visit from IA. However he'd worry about that if—and when--it happened.

Two CSU techs in hazmat suits entered the bullpen and came over to Hanlan's desk with their cases. The techs looked over the desk, then one got to work on it while the other ran a blue light over both detectives.

"Clear," the tech with the light said after he was done with both detectives.

"And I'm done," the other tech said. "Your desk is now clear, Detective."

"Thank you. Your report should go to Detective Howell," Hanlan told them.

Both techs gathered up the evidence and their cases and left.

As the techs went out the front doors, Howell came in. He headed straight for the two detectives and stopped a few feet from them. "Hanlan, Canin."

"Sorry to interrupt your holiday," Hanlan told him.

"I'm not."

"The in-laws getting on your nerves?"

"Just her mother." He sighed, then got serious. "Okay. Canin said the killer sent you another card."

"In an envelope with some kind of powder. I didn't breath any in. I was careful pulling out the card."

Canin retrieved his cell and showed Howell the picture he had snapped before the CSU techs had arrived.

"Right." Howell studied the picture for a minute, then looked at Hanlan as Canin returned his phone to his pocket. "It was in your inbox?"

"Yes."

"I'll have the Desk Sargent pull the video. And I'll have to call the Captain."

"The Captain's coming in tomorrow to talk to us."

"She might pull you," Howell told Hanlan.

"I doubt it. She's getting pressure from the Mayor and the Chief."

"She may suggest a safe house," Canin said.

Hanlan could feel his partner's dissatisfaction at that thought. "She can put a unit outside our apartment if she's worried. I'm not going to some strange safe house."

Canin's cell rang, and he answered with "Canin." He listened for a few minutes, then spoke again. "Okay. We'll be there soon." The phone went back in his pocket, and he looked at Hanlan. "That unit I sent to Davidson's apartment found something they think we should see."

"What?"

"Dispatch didn't say."

Hanlan frowned. His gut was saying this wasn't kosher, but he didn't have a logical reason. "Okay. You want to come with us, Howell?"

"Yeah."

The three detectives left the bullpen and headed toward the elevator. They entered and rode down in silence. The threat was pushed aside for now.

Once outside Hanlan and Canin went to their car and got in while Howell headed for his. They waited until he was ready, then let him follow them to Davidson's apartment.

His apartment turned out to be an old tenement building from the 1960's. Brick and concrete. It was not in good shape. The lobby was in shadow as most of the lights were broken and the stair treads were cracked. They didn't see an elevator.

The detectives went up the stairs to the second floor. There was no sign of the uniforms but the door to 2C was open.

Hanlan dropped back a bit and allowed the other two to enter first. They froze just inside the door and Hanlan moved closer to see what had made them stop.

Two bodies lay on the floor in front of the open window opposite the door. It was the uniform officers by their clothing, but their cheeks had been carved with a Glasgow Smile distorting their faces. A bloody hand print marred one of the dirty window panes and an equally bloody knife was stuck in the wood frame next to it.

However what was holding the detectives' attention was the woman sitting crossways in the open window well.

Kezia James.

Her dark hair was pulled back in a braid and she was wearing a black jumpsuit with a white collar and cuffs. Blood splattered both her and her clothing, but she still looked beautiful. Her olive skin glowed and her dark eyes sparkled above high cheekbones. She burned with vitality. Hanlan could see how most males would be bewitched by her. Yet she did nothing for him as he recognized the sparkle as madness and the flush as dark pleasure and excitement.

"Prastlo." Her voice was husky, almost hypnotic, even though she was glaring at Canin and spat on the floor after she spoke.

"Kezia James, you are under arrest for murder," Canin said as he took a step forward.

Kezia took off through the window onto the fire escape and Canin chased after her while Howell raced out the front door, leaving Hanlan alone in the apartment.

Hanlan had taken a step forward toward the bodies when he suddenly felt a hand on his shoulder, then a sharp pain in his neck. Before he could turn, weakness hit him and he fell to the floor, unable to move. Boots came into his field of vision, then he was lifted and settled over a man's shoulders. The man was wearing a hoodie, so he didn't get a good look at him.

Once the man made sure the detective was secure, he walked out of the apartment and went down the stairs. But instead of going out the front door, the man headed for the basement.

There was a hole in one wall and the man carried Hanlan through it into a dark tunnel. How long they walked Hanlan wasn't sure, but the man suddenly took a turn, and they came out in a dim basement. It was still too dark for Hanlan to see anything but shadows on shadows. The man walked a little more, then lowered Hanlan to the floor.

A loud click brought light. Ten feet away a battery-powered lantern sat on a wooden box with the man squatting beside it. Hanlan still couldn't make out his face though. The area the light encompassed, and Hanlan could see was empty but for the two of them and the lantern.

Kezia materialized out of the darkness and the hooded man stood.

"I brought him like you asked." His voice was a pleasant baritone, but Hanlan caught a hint of something in it. "You promised no more killing."

"It was necessary." Her voice was dismissive. She glided across the floor until she was standing over Hanlan, then dropped to squat beside him. Her dark eyes met Hanlan's.

The madness still glittered there. But like the old saying there was a method to her madness. Hanlan could feel that.

She settled him more firmly on his back, then began to unbutton his shirt.

"Kezia!" the man exclaimed sharply. "You promised."

"It is necessary, Nici. He is interfering in our quest." She undid the last button and uncovered Hanlan's chest before stroking the skin above his heart. Her hand paused though as something tapped the concrete floor near-by.

The tapping came closer, and Kezia jumped to her feet, a knife in her hand. Both she and the man she had called Nici faced the direction the tapping came from.

A dark figure entered the light. He wore a long trench coat with the collar turned up, hiding most of his face, and dark pants tucked in knee boots. In his left hand he carried a walking stick which is where the tapping came from. His hat shadowed his eyes, but they glowed a fiery red, making them stand out in that darkness. He looked like a demon to Hanlan, though the human knew the newcomer was but a Ruv.

"Prastlo," Kezia spat.

"Pikie," the Ruv returned in a pure unaccented voice. "If you leave immediately without the human I won't kill you now."

"He's mine!" Kezia told him as she whirled toward Hanlan.

The man Nici grabbed her and tossed her over his shoulder before disappearing into the darkness.

Hanlan kept his eyes on the Ruv. He didn't sense anything negative coming from him and his gut wasn't nagging. But that didn't mean the Ruv wasn't dangerous. Sometimes Hanlan didn't get a clear read on people. There were those who had such a tight rein on their emotions that he didn't pick up more than a snippet.

"Sunt plina, Shavora," the Ruv told him before turning his head to look into the darkness. "Your Ruv is coming."

Hanlan struggled to speak but all that came out was a hiss of air.

"I am called Patrin," the Ruv said as he disappeared into the darkness. "And you are welcome."

Moments later his partner stepped into the light.

CHAPTER 11

A blanket was wrapped around his shoulders as Hanlan sat on the back of the ambulance with the paramedics fussing about him. By the time it had arrived he had regained the use of his body. Canin had said the enhanced healing he got from being a companion would take care of any remaining stiffness. Had he been a 'normal' human the drug would have probably knocked him unconscious or senseless as well as or instead of paralyzing him. Drugs were tricky things with a companion's metabolism.

Canin was talking with Howell a few feet away. Howell had stayed with the two dead uniforms while Canin had went in search of Hanlan. His partner looked at him and Hanlan motioned for him to come closer. The two detectives came over to where Hanlan was sitting as the paramedics moved away.

"I had to call the Captain." Howell's voice was a bit rueful. "She ought to be here any minute."

Hanlan sighed, then asked, "The officers?"

"CSU is there right now. I can't believe we fell for that trap." Howell shook his head.

"Hindsight."

"Detectives," Captain Gardner said as she joined them. "What's the situation?"

There was silence for a moment, then Hanlan spoke. "We were told that our presence was required by the unit we sent to the apartment that Davidson shared with one of our suspects in his murder. When we arrived, we found the officers dead and the suspect present. It seems it was all a trap to get me though as she did a runner, pulling Howell and Canin away so her accomplice could snatch me."

"Accomplice?"

"I suspect it's her brother," Hanlan told her.

"A family affair."

"Yes. Canin found me before anything could happen."

The Captain transferred her gaze to Canin.

"When I lost her and returned to find Hanlan gone, I searched the building. The basement first and found the egress. I followed the main tunnel for a while, looking for any sign of passage. I was about to give up when I heard voices."

"They must have heard him because they left rather abruptly."

"You were all rather reckless." The captain frowned at them.

"I'm not going to hide." Hanlan frowned back at her. "And I'm not letting this keep me from the case."

"I think that's my decision," she told him.

Hanlan just stared at her. He was going to work the case with or without her permission. It would just be easier with.

She sighed and pinched her nose between her eyes. "Detective Canin, you are not to leave your partner's side. Am I clear?"

"Yes, ma'am."

"Detective Howell, you and your partner will stay assigned to the case with Hanlan and Canin. I'll pull you from the rotation until this is resolved."

Howell nodded.

"Thank you, Captain."

"Go home, Hanlan," the captain told him. "Howell can handle this for now."

The detective shoved off the blanket and stood. He stretched a bit, then moved away from the ambulance. With a nod to Howell and the captain, he and Canin headed toward where he had parked the car earlier.

"You going to let me drive?" Canin asked.

"Nope."

"Didn't think so."

As soon as they got to the car, they slid into their usual places. Hanlan drove away, heading for their apartment. Neither spoke for a while, then Hanlan asked, "What does sunt plina mean besides the obvious 'I am full'?"

Canin looked at him sharply. "Who said that to you?"

"What does it mean?" he repeated.

"When a Ruv says it it's a promise that you are safe from them. They mean you no harm. Comes from the idea they have already satisfied their bloodthirst."

"Ah."

The rest of the drive was conducted in silence. Hanlan parked in his spot, then sat there, staring out the windshield, while Canin watched him.

"What happened in that basement?" Canin asked.

Hanlan sighed and opened the car door. "I'll tell you inside."

Both detectives got out of the car and headed to the entryway. Hanlan unlocked the door, and they went inside the apartment. After re-locking the door, Hanlan headed into the living room while Canin went to the refrigerator.

His jacket was tossed onto a chair as Hanlan moved by it toward the bathroom. He made a pit stop, then went back out to the living room to collapse on the sofa.

Canin handed him a beer, then settled on the sofa next to him.

Hanlan took a long swallow of beer, then rested the bottle on the sofa arm. He stared at the bottle as he spoke. "Kezia and her brother were arguing about killing me. He didn't want her to, but he wasn't stopping her either."

His partner reached out and laid a hand on Hanlan's thigh. The comfort was more for the Ruv than for Hanlan, he knew.

"A Ruv appeared."

"One of Phuro's enforcers?"

"I don't know. He said his name was Patrin."

Canin tensed and Hanlan felt a flare of emotion, but Canin suppressed it before Hanlan could name it. "What did he look like?"

"I couldn't see his face. He was wearing a dark trench coat with the collar up and a hat pulled down, but his eyes were glowing red. Literally."

"He was the one who told you sunt plina?"

"Yes. Who is he?"

"Mulo."

"A spirit of the dead?" Hanlan raised an eyebrow as he looked at Canin. The Ruv had seemed real enough, glowing eyes notwithstanding.

Canin sat his beer on the coffee table, then got up from the sofa and headed for the chair with Hanlan's jacket on it. He picked up the jacket and pulled out the mulengi dori, letting the jacket fall back on the chair while he stared at the knotted string. "A mule-vi must have prepared this."

"You're telling me ghosts are real?"

"Our version of them anyway." Canin returned to the sofa and set the mulengi dori on the coffee table before settling back next to Hanlan.

Before either of them could say anything more, a knock sounded on the back door. They looked at each other for a minute, then Canin got up and went to answer it.

Hanlan took another swig of beer, keeping his eyes on the kitchen archway as he waited. He felt a jolt of surprise from Canin, so he was apprehensive when his partner returned with their guests.

Lupo and her assistant Ms. Croft stopped just inside the doorway from the kitchen. Canin took a few more steps, then turned sideways to stand part way between them and Hanlan.

"What are you doing here?" Hanlan got straight to the point.

As did Lupo. "If anyone is going to kill you it will be me."

"Julia," Croft hissed.

Lupo was unrepentant.

"Why are you here?" Hanlan asked again. He knew where he stood with her, so he was unsurprised by her statement, just her presence.

"This human has butted in where she has no business. You have two days to handle it, or I'll do it myself."

"I'm surprised you haven't already."

Lupo looked sideways at Croft who stared back at her squarely with a raised eyebrow.

Canin's eyes flickered back and forth between the two for a second, then he blurted out, "She's your Shavora!"

Hanlan frowned. "I thought you said Shavora were male."

"Usually male," Canin corrected.

"I'm not her Shavora," Croft told them, a touch of wistfulness in her voice. "I am her kumpanija though. Wortacha or partners it may be said."

Hanlan stared at her for a moment, then told her, "you are destined to fail. Her obsession and nature is too strong. Be careful that you are not consumed as well."

Croft gave him a defiant look.

"Just a warning. Your choice." He held up his hands briefly to her before turning his attention back to the glaring Lupo. "You should keep out of this."

Lupo's eyes flared topaz as she glared harder at him.

Canin growled a warning.

"It's alright, pral," Hanlan told his partner before speaking to Lupo again. "You have said your peace, now leave my home."

"Two days," Lupo reminded him before escorting her assistant toward the back door with Canin following behind them.

Hanlan took another sip of his beer, then let his head drop to the back of the sofa and stared vacantly at the ceiling. He heard Canin enter after a while but didn't move, then the sofa cushions shifted as Canin sat beside him moments later. Tapping reached his ears and he asked, "Phuro?"

"Yes. He needs to know what she's said."

"But he probably won't do anything to keep her out of this, will he?"

There was silence for a moment, then Canin said, "He might want to send his enforcers after James and her brother since they threaten the safety of the Lexicon."

"But not because they kidnapped me."

Another silence, then, "That would be for me to balance."

"Cause we're not members of the Pack."

"Yes."

Hanlan sighed. "She didn't have to kill those officers."

"No, it was not necessary to her trap."

Even though he knew it was not his fault Hanlan still felt guilt about the officers death. It had been a trap for him after all. Logic didn't invalidate, erase or change emotion. And time didn't heal all wounds. Some remained an open part of you and dictated how you acted from there on. Witness him and relationships.

The sofa shifted and a heavy head settled in his lap as Canin laid down. Hanlan's free hand reached down, and he scratched between Canin's two ears. The Ruv knew Hanlan was more comfortable taking solace from the wolf, then the human him. More of his human baggage.

They sat there in silence for a while, Hanlan sipping his beer and petting Canin. Canin finally shimmered, returning to his human form, and Hanlan allowed his hand to rest on his partner's chest.

"It wouldn't do any good to make anything, would it?" Canin asked.

"No." Hanlan removed his hand from his partner's chest so he could sit up.

Canin swung his feet to the floor, then stood up. He grabbed the two bottles, one still full and one empty, and headed for the kitchen. Within seconds he was back and offered his hand to Hanlan. "Let's go to bed."

"You'll keep the nightmares away?" Hanlan asked, taking the hand.

"Don't I always?"

CHAPTER 12

Breakfast was pancakes, eggs, and sausage. And Canin told him he was to eat all of it. The Ruv hadn't liked that he'd missed supper, even though he understood why.

Hanlan sat down and got to work on the plate of food. He had woken up wrapped again in Canin's embrace. For a few minutes he had allowed himself the comfort, then had gotten out of bed as his partner woke up. His emotions concerning the Ruv were confused, and he kept them mostly locked away. He was too old and had had enough emotional bloodletting in his life for him to have a crisis of any kind now as far as he was concerned. Besides he might as well be asexual for all that he didn't physically react to Canine's touch/embrace.

"I ran a google search on Croft Manor while you were in the shower," Canin told Hanlan as they both ate. "It was built by Richard Croft back in 1910. He was the local railway baron. The Manor was his retirement home. His wife, who was ten years his junior, led a varied social life but he was an invalid. According to what I read he was confined upstairs while his wife partied downstairs. I didn't find anything interesting in the rest of its past."

"Brennon would have said something if there had been." Hanlan pushed away his empty plate and took a sip of his coffee. "I wonder if Ms. Croft is related."

"I'll check that out when we get to the station." Canin finished his breakfast, then stood and gathered the plates to take them to the sink. "Don't forget we have a meeting at the Manor with Ms. Rose at 9 a.m."

"The recent events haven't messed with my memory, thank you very much," Hanlan said.

Canin turned from putting the plates down and raised his hands briefly in surrender before rinsing and setting the dishes on the drainer. He poured two travel mugs of coffee, then reset the machine.

Hanlan joined him and set his coffee cup in the sink, then grabbed a mug as he turned to head to the back door. He went into the back entry room as Canin did his last rounds of the apartment and waited for his partner to finish.

After Canin joined Hanlan, the detectives went out and got in the car. They drove to the station in silence. Once there, Hanlan parked in his normal spot, and they headed inside.

"Hanlan," Reach called before they could head to the elevator.

The two detectives came over to the caged window.

"I heard about your 'gift'." Reach got straight to the point. "You'd be interested to know that the chief investigator of the Laney murders received one as well before he disappeared."

"Disappeared?" Hanlan frowned. "I didn't see that or anything about receiving a threat anywhere in the file."

"He was a known alcoholic, and they contributed his disappearance to that. His partner took over and the investigation stalled."

"Can't be the same killer. She's not old enough."

"Father--or mother, maybe. Just be careful. You've already been snatched once."

Hanlan nodded. "Thanks for the info," he told Reach before he and Canin turned toward the elevator.

The two detectives got into the elevator and rode it to the fourth floor. When the doors opened they walked out and headed to the bullpen. Their captain was waiting at their desks for them when they arrived there. She was holding two files against her chest and watched them sit with narrowed eyes.

"Are those the official autopsy reports?" Hanlan asked, looking back at her.

She stared at him for another minute, then nodded. "Yes. And CSU left a copy of their initial report on the items found in your entryway. I put a rush on it."

Hanlan glanced at his inbox and saw the new

file. "Excellent." He reached out a hand for the files she held, and after a moment she gave them to him. Setting them on his desk, he raised an eyebrow at her. "Anything else, Captain?"

Gardner looked at both of them hard. "Watch your backs."

"He ain't getting out of my sight again," Canin promised.

"Good. Now get this person." She spun on her heels and headed for her office.

Hanlan opened the top file and flipped through it until he came to the tox panel. He paused for a moment, then opened the other file and went to the tox panel findings there as well. "Same paralytic as in the Laney murders."

"If CSU finds the same in the blood sample you allowed them to take, then James is either a copycat with inside knowledge or..." Canin broke off.

"I think Reach has the right of it. One or both of her parents killed the Laneys. The Cult notwithstanding." He paused. "You sure CSU won't find anything else suspicious in my blood?"

"Just an unusual amount of white blood cells and proteins. Their tests aren't looking for the right things." He slid up to his computer and started typing.

"Okay." Hanlan closed the files, then reached for the folder in his inbox and pulled it out. He opened it and glanced through it. "They also think the heart came from Davidson. They're running DNA."

"Good." He paused. "I'm catching up our notes. Howell's handling the threats and kidnapping, right?"

"Yeah."

Howell and Deneque chose that moment to join them. Deneque was frowning and Howell was patting his shoulder. They obviously had been talking about something that was upsetting to Deneque.

"I brought him up-to-date," Howell said.

"There appears to be a similar murder case like the Ruthridge's," Hanlan told them. "1989. The Laneys. Same M.O. And the lead investigator got the same gift before he disappeared."

Howell was frowning now.

"We figure it's some Cult thing," Canin added. "Initiation of a new generation perhaps."

Hanlan's phone rang and he answered with his normal, "Hanlan." He listened for a few minutes, then said, "Thank you," before hanging up. "That was the lab. They'll have the Ruthridge forensic report to us by 1 p.m. but they wanted us to know the single strand of long dark hair they had found sequenced human and female. And it wasn't Mrs. Ruthridge's."

"So they have DNA from the killer," Howell said. "They going to run it against James'?"

"Her DNA isn't on file, but they are running DNA from Davidson's apartment and they're sure they'll get hers," Hanlan told him.

"I thought Canin told me she had priors." Howell was frowning again.

"But nothing violent so no DNA in the System."

"We'll come back after lunch," Canin commented. "But we need to get going soon to meet the book expert at Croft Manor."

Hanlan nodded, then glanced at the clock before he and Canin stood. "We'll conference later," he told Howell.

Howell inclined his head to Hanlan, then pulled Deneque with him as he left.

Hanlan and Canin headed out. It was a little early, but they both didn't want to answer too many questions about Kezia James. The detectives rode the elevator down in silence. Reach wasn't at his desk, so they continued on out the door with no interruption. They got into the car and Hanlan drove them away toward Croft Manor.

"Do you know this prophecy Rose mentioned?" Hanlan suddenly asked.

"I know a lot of the legends as I told you, but I never heard of a prophecy."

Anything Hanlan would have said was stalled as they pulled into the Manor and saw the sight before them.

A Trust van was parked behind Rose's car and two men, and a woman was standing by her driver door. Hanlan recognized the auburn-haired woman and hurriedly parked. He and Canin got out and rushed toward them. One of the men was grabbing the door handle while reaching in the open window with the other hand when they arrived behind the group.

"What's happening here?" Hanlan asked in a harsh voice.

"This doesn't concern you, Detective," Assistant Director Cowen said, her green eyes not leaving Rose.

The man continued to unlock the door and open

it before pulling Rose out of her car forcefully. Rose jerked her arm out of his hand and stood glaring as Hanlan took a step closer.

"Assaulting her does concern me."

Cowen stared into Rose's hazel eyes with a frown for a moment, then motioned her men back before telling Rose, "there's been a misunderstanding." She gestured to her men, and they all headed to the van. One man slid in the driver side while she and the other man got in the back.

Hanlan held his tongue until the van disappeared out the gate. "Whomever told her about you didn't have the full story or didn't tell her."

"Nope." She closed her car door and slipped her keys into her pants pocket. "And she's going to let her displeasure be known. I could almost feel sorry."

Canin grunted.

"I said 'Almost'. Shall we?" She nodded toward the Manor.

The three of them walked up the pathway to the door where Hanlan unlocked it and motioned the others in. After they entered, Hanlan followed them inside and re-locked the door. They headed up the stairs to the second floor, then went into the library. It was still a mess as the scene had not been released yet.

Rose carefully righted one of the chairs and sat down, her eyes scanning the room. "Whomever did this obviously doesn't know what the Lexicon looks like."

Hanlan and Canin set up their own chairs and sat

facing Rose.

"Right," she said as soon as they settled. "The prophecy. It begins and ends with the Shavora. Our fate has always been in their hands. That the Ruv have forgotten that is shameful."

"Shavora are respected," Canin said.

"Not the way they should be. Do you think Ulven would give his life for you and your Shavora?"

Canin frowned.

"Shavora bonded are sacred," Rose continued when Canin didn't answer. "The misinterpretation of the prophecy, fear, and plain old envy has led to the lessening of the respect Shavora deserve over the centuries. I will be correcting that."

"I have a feeling that won't make you popular with the other Ruv," Hanlan told her.

"I don't need to be popular."

"You'll be challenged," Canin said.

"Perhaps." There was a strange smile on her face for a moment, then she got serious. "Now the prophecy. It is believed a Chosen will betray the Ruv, allowing the Hunters to wipe out all of us. A good deal are afraid that the Chosen would be a Shavora, thus privy to our vulnerabilities. Elders like Ulven have access to the original translation."

"But it's negative or he wouldn't be so apprehensive," Hanlan said.

"It shows a vulnerability and dependence on those who are essentially human and a lot of Ruv don't like that. But we are as we are because of Shavora so it is just that Shavora decide our fate."

"You seem to be delaying telling us the prophecy

itself," Hanlan told her. "Which makes it seem not good."

"There will come a Raven with the 'gift' who will bond with a broken Ruv. Their Shavora bond will out shine the moon with its power. However forces will try to break that bond through death. The gifted Raven is the key to the future of the Del Mulanti Ruv and should the Raven fall so too will the Ruv." She paused, allowing the words to sink in a bit before she continued. "Hunters would ravish, and every human hand would be against those of the bloodlines. Chaos would rule the sundered world. You can see why Ulven would be apprehensive."

"He knows this wording of the prophecy?" Canin asked. His eyes narrowed as he looked at her.

"Each translation is different because of the translator's interpretation of the words. What I have said is what it was meant to mean but sequential translations have changed what the prophecy is told to say. Which presently is a doomsday betrayal by a Shavora."

"So that's why he acts the way he does around me," Hanlan said. "He fears I'm the embodiment of this recent prophecy."

"And he doesn't know which is truth." Rose nodded. "Though he has seen the original translation, he has been surrounded and inundate with the various versions. So he is ambivalent."

Canin let out an angry sound as he scowled. "That's a word for it."

"Why don't you two take an early lunch and think on this, then come back later this afternoon? I should have this straightened up by then."

"You really going to go through these books?" Hanlan asked.

"Yes," she said with a smile. "Can't think of anything more I'd like to do."

Hanlan studied her face. She was telling the truth. Shelving these books wasn't a job to her but a pleasure. "You sure you'll be okay after what happened earlier?"

"She won't bother me again. Things weren't what she thought to her mind, so I have no qualms about being here alone."

"Okay." He stood up and Canin followed suite. "Do you plan to work straight through?"

"I brought a sandwich and water. They're in the car."

He nodded, then he and Canin headed for the door. "I'll lock the deadbolt behind us, just in case."

Rose slid off the chair and knelt, reaching for a book, already dismissing them.

The two detectives looked at each other for a second, then left the room.

CHAPTER 13

Lunch was actually a quiet affair.

They had decided to discuss what they had learned when they got home that evening. No chance of eavesdroppers. Also both needed to come to terms within themselves before they talked with each other about it.

Hanlan was mostly in denial. His great-grandmother had called him her little raven. But that didn't mean he was the raven in the prophecy nor Canin the broken Ruv. Why would the fate of an entire race be set in his hands? Had to be a misunderstanding somewhere. He shoved it all into a box in his head and closed the lid. It wouldn't stay there he knew but they needed to concentrate on the murders right now.

The forensic report was waiting for them in Hanlan's inbox when they returned to the bullpen. Both detectives sat at their desks before Hanlan retrieved the file. As he looked through it, Howell and Deneque joined them and stood waiting.

"None of the fingerprints were usable. Not enough detail. The footprints are more consistent with a woman's than a man's. No foreign DNA except the single strand of hair." He summarized. "They went over everything twice."

"In other words nothing forensically speaking except the DNA," Howell said, showing a bit of frustration.

"Hopefully they'll do better with the Davidson scene and his apartment." Hanlan closed the file and threw it on his desk. "How is your end coming?"

"The lab is still running tests. So as I said nothing forensically speaking."

"Just keep me in the loop, okay?" Hanlan looked at Howell.

"I will." Howell met his eyes. They stared at each other for a moment, then Howell shifted his eyes to Canin. "You might need to put a leash on him. He's slippery."

Canin cracked a smile and Hanlan felt the grim humor his partner experienced at the words. "I thought about it."

Hanlan knew he hadn't because of who and what his partner was. Collaring was the most vile thing you could do to a Ruv. Caging was second. But Hanlan was sure handcuffing Hanlan to something had crossed his partner's mind as least once. "Hey!"

Howell raised his hands in surrender as he

smiled. "Just saying." He grew serious though in the next moment. "I drew up your statement. You'll need to sign it when you can."

Hanlan nodded. He dreaded reading it, but he knew it had to be done. Though it wasn't the full truth. Some things like the mulo had to be kept out. Especially if he wanted to keep the case—and his job.

A uniform dropped a manila envelope on Hanlan's desk and Hanlan straightened in his chair. He slipped on a pair of latex gloves he pulled from his right drawer, then reached for the envelope. His name was scrawled on it but no address like the other envelope from the killer. "Catch him," Hanlan told Deneque.

The detective nodded and took off after the uniform.

Hanlan opened the envelope with a pen knife from his middle drawer and carefully drew out the paper inside. It was written in what looked like blood in calligraphy style. "Sorry our meeting was cut short. I really had looked forward to getting to know you better. I would in truth love to have a second chance to continue our talk. In the meantime we each have a job to do. See you soon." He paused. "She signed it with two symbols. The ones from the Laney murders."

Deneque had returned while Hanlan was talking. "She wouldn't have even been more than a baby," he said now.

"No." Hanlan looked at him. "Did anyone see who left it?"

"The Desk Sargent said it was there when he

came back from lunch. His relief said he just turned around and it was there on the desk. I told them to pull the footage."

"Good." He laid the paper down and looked inside the envelope before tilting it up and shaking it. A tarot card fell out. Another death card with a slit in the center. "She is consistent."

A CSU tech appeared, and Hanlan raised an eyebrow.

"I called them," Deneque said.

Hanlan nodded, then gestured to the stuff on his desk, scooting back a little.

The CSU tech pulled on his own gloves, then carefully picked up the items and put them in the evidence bags he had brought with him. "You're popular," he commented as he worked. Once he had the bags sealed and gathered, he looked at Howell. "I'll get right on this."

Howell nodded and the tech left as the detective turned his attention back to Hanlan. "Sounds like she plans to finish what she started with you and soon."

"After she does this 'job' she mentioned, it seems."

"Whatever it is she must be near to finishing it," Deneque said. "At least it sounds that way."

Canin frowned and his brows drew together.

"Did you find out what those words sprawled on the wall mean?" Howell asked. "Maybe they'll give us a clue to the killer's agenda."

"Not yet," Canin said before Hanlan could speak. "Still haven't heard back from the language expert."

"From the state of the Ruthridge's library I'd say

the killer was looking for a book." Deneque paused. "And it must have more than monetary value."

"At least to the killer," Hanlan said.

"You still looking into the cult angle?" Howell asked.

"Yes." Canin answered again before Hanlan could say anything. "With the symbols linking this killer with the Laney murders it's becoming more likely."

"We should probably meet back up with Ms. Rose at Croft Manor," Hanlan said as he scooted his chair back and stood. "Keep us in the loop," he told Howell.

"You do the same," replied Howell. He and Deneque turned and headed back to their desks.

Canin got up and slid his chair in under his desk.

Hanlan looked at him and raised an eyebrow, waiting.

His partner grimaced. "Later."

"Alright." Hanlan let him off the hook for now, but he would get an answer later.

The detectives left the bullpen and headed to the elevator. They rode down in silence, but it was a comfortable quiet with nothing on their minds. Once in the back lobby, they glanced over to see an empty desk through the window so continued on out. At the car, they got in, then Hanlan drove away. It didn't take Hanlan long to get to Croft Manor and he parked in the drive not far behind Rose's car.

Rose was leaning against her car but straightened when the two detectives approached. She tilted her head as she regarded them. "Something happened," she stated.

"Another threat from the killer." Canin's voice was nearly a growl.

Rose looked at Hanlan.

Hanlan nodded.

"And what is Ulven doing about this?" she demanded.

"She is pikie already," Canin said.

Her eyes narrowed. "This is unacceptable."

Canin merely stared back at her.

She shook her head, then made a gesture toward the Manor. "I looked through the books. There is one missing from the auction lot, a leather-bound tome of Old- World folktales."

"Folktales?" Hanlan asked.

"What we would call urban legends. It was a beautifully tooled book and worth quite a bit."

"I doubt she wanted it for the worth."

"Perhaps not. But maybe for the content or even its look."

"Okay." He glanced toward the Manor, then dug out the keys and tossed them to Canin. "Since she's done, lock it up."

Canin glanced at both of them, then turned and headed toward the front door.

Rose raised an eyebrow at Hanlan.

"You seem to know more about the Ruv's past than Phuro or any of the other Ruv."

"My family was a part of that past and we never forgot our roots. There's been willful forgetting because of shame and arrogance. But it's time to put that behind. Our enemies have grown stronger, and we can't afford that ignorance and division anymore."

"You're not going to be popular."

"As I have said before, I'm not here to be popular."

Canin rejoined them and tossed the keys back to Hanlan. "Back to the station?"

"Yes," he told his partner, then looked back at Rose. "Thank you for speaking frankly with me." He gave Canin a sideways look. "Something others seem to have problems with."

Rose frowned at Canin. "He doesn't speak truthfully with you?" she asked Hanlan.

"He doesn't lie to me, but he also doesn't tell me everything."

Her frown deepened as she stared hard at Canin. "There should be no holding back or secrets between you and your Shavora."

Canin ducked his head and Hanlan could feel the turmoil of his emotions.

"I know you both have been hurt, but you can heal each other."

Hanlan felt his own flare of uncomfortable emotions but suppressed it. Whatever else, he wanted to make this relationship work and he felt he couldn't do that if Canin kept holding back. Made it hard for him to trust.

"The bond will suffer as will you both if either of you hold back." She looked at both of them, then sighed and opened her car door. "I'm going to have a word with Ulven. He needs to step up."

"Good luck with that," Hanlan told her.

"Luck won't have anything to do with it." She slid into the car and slammed the door as she spoke, anger radiating from her.

Hanlan was glad he wasn't the Ruv elder.

The detectives stepped away from the car and Rose sped away with a spray of gravel. Both of them headed back to their vehicle, then got in and drove away themselves.

CHAPTER 14

As soon as Hanlan and Canin sat down at their desks, Howell and Deneque came over, Howell holding a file. "Forensics on your 'gift' came in while you were gone," he said as he tapped the folder.

Both Hanlan and Canin raised an eyebrow. "That was fast," Hanlan said.

Howell waved that away and continued. "They found foreign DNA on the handle. It was female so they compared it to the foreign hair from the Ruthridge scene and got a match. But no match in CODIS."

"Kezia James," Canin stated.

"They still don't have her DNA so they can't commit to that."

"The BOLOs?" Hanlan asked.

"Haven't turned up anything yet."

"What else is in the report?"

"They got DNA from the blood and the heart. Same person for both. Just need something to compare it to. The tarot card is old style but readily available at several shops. And the knife is a popular one used by hunters. Nothing to make either unique or easy to trace."

"So nothing probative but the DNA." Hanlan frowned, a line etched between his brows.

"Gentlemen," the captain said as she joined them. "The Mayor called again, wanting an update."

"We don't have much new information," Hanlan told her. "Forensics are still out on a few things. But DNA was matched to both the Ruthridge murders and my 'gift'. However no positive ID to Kezia James as we don't have her DNA on file and no match in CODIS."

The Captain frowned. "Nothing else?"

"Not as of now." Hanlan shook his head. "The BOLOS haven't turned up anything yet either." He paused. "What have you heard about the officers?"

"IA is still doing their investigation." The Captain looked at Howell and raised an eyebrow.

"The M.E. was to do the autopsies today," he told her. "And the lab's still working on the evidence."

Gardner nodded in acknowledgment, then looked at Hanlan. "You and your partner get out of here."

Hanlan heaved himself up with a sigh and Canin stood as well.

"Normally I'd assign a car to watch your place or

send you to a safe house," she said but held up her hands to stop Hanlan's protest. "But I know you. You and your partner are to be joined at the hip, do I make myself clear?"

"Yes." Hanlan grumbled, but he was actually grateful that she trusted him and Canin enough to allow this.

"Don't make me regret this, Detectives." She glared at them for a moment, then gestured. "Now go home."

Both of them nodded to her, then turned and headed for the door.

"See you in the morning," Howell called after them.

Hanlan waved his hand before they disappeared out of the bullpen. In moments they were in the elevator, and they rode down in silence.

As soon as they stepped into the back lobby, Reach called them over.

"You have something for us?" Hanlan asked as soon as he and his partner joined Reach at the window.

"Rumors mostly. But I figured you'd want to hear them." He paused and Hanlan nodded. "The Trust is in a flurry. Cowen and Deneque both are hunting your killer but separately. And it's said for different reasons."

Hanlan frowned. "And?"

"The rumor is that Cowen wants an alliance with the killer, Deneque to get rid of a complication."

"Is there any indication that they know who it is?" Canin asked.

"No." Reach shook his head. "But I'd watch my

six if I was you. They may be watching you and we know they wouldn't hesitate to kill you both."

"Thanks for the info." Hanlan stepped back and Canin followed.

"Be careful."

Hanlan nodded, then the two detectives headed for the back door. Once outside they went down the stairs and over to the car. They got in the vehicle and minutes later Hanlan drove away from the station. On the way home, they stopped at a drive-thru burger place for supper as neither of them felt like cooking.

As soon as they arrived at the apartment, Canin grabbed their food and followed his partner to the entrance. They both checked around for any more surprises before Hanlan unlocked the door and they entered. Once inside the door was re-locked and the detectives headed for the kitchen table. Canin detoured long enough to start the coffee maker, then joined Hanlan at the table. Both sat down and retrieved their food from the bag.

"When I ask questions, you deflect or tell me very little." Hanlan didn't look up from his food as he spoke. "Do you not trust me?"

"More than I trust myself."

Hanlan could feel the sincerity of Canin's words as well as some sadness. "Then why don't you talk to me?"

"I can feel you holding back."

The words were softly spoken, but they struck Hanlan like a knife. He closed his eyes for a second, then snapped them open to look at Canin with determination. "What you feel as me holding back is me not trusting myself or life itself. I'm waiting for the other shoe to drop. I..." he broke off as he struggled with himself to voice what he was feeling.

Canin stood, then tugged Hanlan to his feet before wrapping his partner in a hug.

Hanlan was tense for a few seconds, then melted against his partner. The comfort was too good to pass up, no matter his conflicting impulses. Canin had eroded most the societal conditioning of male touch this past month and Hanlan liked the feelings he got when Canin touched him. There was nothing sexual about it. Pleasure, comfort, and intimacy wasn't only about sex. He was learning that.

Canin's cell rang, and he carefully retrieved it one-handedly without releasing Hanlan. "Canin."

There was a pause and Hanlan felt Canin tense. He raised his head from Canin's neck and shoulder then took a step back, his partner letting him go.

"Where?" Another pause. "We'll be there in fifteen." Canin tapped the phone, then put it away. "We got more bodies."

"Bodies? As in more than one?" He pushed his emotions back down and put on his cop face. They would have to continue this later.

"Three to be exact." Canin gathered up their trash and left-over food as he spoke, then put them in either the garbage can or refrigerator. "I'll be ready in five."

Hanlan did a pit stop in the bathroom as Canin did his round of the apartment and they met at the back door. After ensuring the door was locked, they went to the car and got in with Hanlan asking, "Where to?"

"National Park."

He knew it well. It was a wooded park that straddled two precincts and not a place to be at night. He'd had many calls from there.

It only took him ten minutes to get them there as the evening traffic was light tonight. But as he pulled in behind a patrol car, he was uneasy.

No one was in sight and the lights at the beginning of the walkway through the trees was out. The woods were also dark and still.

Both detectives stayed in the car.

"Another trap, you think?" Hanlan asked.

Suddenly there was movement in the trees and a wavering light appeared.

"Canin?"

"It's an officer," Canin told him.

Hanlan let out the breath he had been holding unconsciously, then they both got out of the vehicle. The detective was surprised to see that the uniform was Davidson's partner O'Malley. He should have been off-duty hours ago. "O'Malley," Hanlan called softly as the uniform made it to the patrol car.

O'Malley startled a bit, then said, "Oh, Detectives."

His mind had obviously been on something else, or he would have seen them and their car. Hanlan frowned at him. "Where are the others?" He gestured to the nearly deserted dimly lit parking lot.

"Oh, they parked at the Thompson street entrance. Most people use that egress to access the park. Only us old timers use this lot."

"I see." Only his car and the patrol car were the only vehicles in this lot. "Is CSU and the M.E. with the bodies?" he asked, getting back to business.

"Yes."

"Did you see any evidence of the killer on your way to and from the scene?"

"The pathway's cement not gravel so I didn't expect to."

Hanlan nodded, then gestured for Canin to follow and moved toward the pathway.

The slightly curving pathway through the trees was dimly lit and dusk hovered just outside the lights and grass strip. They made sure to stay on the path as they headed deeper into the park. A raven sat on one of the benches they passed that were placed along the way and its eyes glittered at them as they passed. It was the only sign of life they had seen since they'd entered.

Brighter light suddenly shone ahead, and they hurried their pace.

Two banks of portable lights lit the area around a bench and another bank was set shining back into the woods. Doctor Brennon and her two assistants with the stretcher were by the bench and three CSIs were moving back and forth between the bench and the woods.

The detectives headed toward the M.E..

A partially dressed body was sprawled across the bench. His shirt and jacket had been sliced off to expose his chest which had been cut open and had organs removed.

When he saw the face, Hanlan paused for a moment, then continued to Brennon's side. "Brennon."

"Detectives," the M.E. greeted them both.

"What do we have?"

"Mr. Richard Barrington. I found a needle mark in the neck. Like the others he was alive when he was carved up so I'm sure the cause will be the same. But until I do the autopsy I can't say for sure."

"I was told there were three bodies," Canin said.

"The other two are over there." Brennon gestured into the woods where the light bank was. "Looks like there was some kind of fight."

Hanlan raised an eyebrow.

"Different injuries and no mutilation."

Canin went to check out the other bodies.

Before Hanlan could ask Brennon any questions, Canin called for him. "I'll be right back," he told Brennon before going to join his partner. He glanced at the grim-faced Ruv before looking at the bodies.

Both men were lying on their backs with their shirts sliced open. Bruises marred their faces and necks and blood puddled under their lower backs. It took him awhile with the bruising, but Hanlan finally recognized them. They were the two men that had been with Director Deneque in the library the other day.

"Do you think Deneque was here?" Hanlan asked Canin in a low voice. "That he was meeting Barrington?"

"I don't know. But why was Barrington here?"

The two detectives went back to Brennon.

"You find identification with those two?" Hanlan asked her.

"Driver licenses and membership cards for the

Alsena Historical Society and Trust were found next to them with empty wallets."

"The names?"

"Alex Jensen and John Hansen."

"Cause of death?"

"It looks like they were both stabbed and strangled but I won't know for sure what actually killed them until I do an autopsy."

"And when do you think that will be?"

"I'll try to get started before lunch tomorrow. But I have two other bodies to do first before I can start on these. It's still only been Anderson and I."

"They still haven't replaced Anstrom? He's been gone six months!"

"Don't I know it."

Hanlan shook his head. "Gotta love bureaucracy." He glanced down at the body, then looked at Brennon again. "Get me the report as soon as you can."

Brennon nodded in acknowledgment before gesturing her assistants to the body.

Both detectives turned and walked back down the pathway. They were silent until the scene was out of sight behind them.

"She must have been interrupted or she would have cut them too."

Canin nodded. "It's part of her madness. She can't help herself."

"Obsession led to madness, yet there is still the purpose."

"Sounds like a quote," Canin told him.

"It is. From a profiler I worked with a long time ago."

They came out of the park and into the dimly lit parking lot. The patrol car was of course gone so it was empty except for their vehicle. Canin glanced around as they continued to the car, his eyes lingering on a spot nearby before roving the lot again. They got in and Hanlan drove them away, heading back home.

CHAPTER 15

Once they got home, they settled into the living room, Hanlan on the couch and Canin in a chair facing him. They were silent for a while, as each sorted their thoughts.

"Let's put aside the case for a moment. We need to clear the air." Hanlan said suddenly.

"What do you want to know?" Canin asked.

"Everything."

"That's a tall order," Canin told him. "My people have over seven thousand years of co-existing and hiding among humans. You have to be more specific."

"More about your race and companions—Shavora, then. You only give me tidbits."

"Because that's all we know about our own

history, though ones like Phuro are researching it more. As to Shavora," he paused. "Each family unit and Pack have their own stories. Shavora are the other half of our souls. They keep us from going rogue, but they are rare. Though many of us have humans like Lupo who we treasure just as much."

"Phuro doesn't seem to 'treasure' Shavora."

"The last few centuries rumors have circulated that the Shavora will bring death and destruction to us. Now that I've heard of the prophecy that may be the basis of the rumors."

"Fear can cause a lot of things."

His partner nodded.

A knock sounded at the back door and with a glance at Hanlan, Canin got up to answer it.

Hanlan watched him head into the kitchen, then shifted so he could get to his weapon if he had to. Night visitors weren't always welcome guests.

Canin returned with two visitors, Phuro and Rose. He moved to stand beside Hanlan while the other two settled in the chairs.

Phuro looked irritated while Rose was poker-faced.

"To what do we owe this visit?" Hanlan asked.

"I thought it a good idea to clear a few things up. Ignorance is not bliss or acceptable." Rose threw Phuro a look before leaning forward. "Let's go back to the beginning. There were many beings living on this planet, beings that humans only know through fairy tales now. We'll call them the Immortals. While the Immortals reproduced slowly, the humans breed faster and spread far and wide. They grew greedy, envious of the older beings who though smaller in population were prosperous with other things. Instead of learning how to flourish on their own, they decided to take. A few humans sided with the Immortals, and many died because of that decision by the hands of some of their own. The dragons and those that would become the Ruv retreated into their lands becoming hunted fugitives, then legends but still hunted.

Without the Roma, the Ruv would not have survived."

Phuro leaned forward and opened his mouth, but a look from Rose had him close it and remain silent.

"We were wanderers so who, but other outcast wanderers would understand us. By that time we were few and far between, but the Roma took us in and hid us. Some died by Hunters' hands for doing so as at that time we were hard to mistake for regular wolves. By appearance we were a cross between a sloth and a wolf. Something had to be done or we would cease to exist. The Elders prayed for a solution and finally we were given one." She paused. "The Gods performed blood-magic on us, using Roma blood as the base, and gave us the ability to shift to human form while changing our natural form to more canine in appearance. We also got the ability for energy manipulation. But that was not all it did. It also gave us something negative."

"The Madness," Canin murmured.

"Yes. The Gods gave us Shavora to combat that and to bring us contentment. Friendships may bring us happiness, but only Shavora give us true contentment."

"How did we lose this knowledge? Why were we

left ignorant as you say?" Phuro asked.

"There is always a cost. Many of the Ruv were willing to pay with ignorance for a chance at safety. Only the Oru remembered as they were given the guardianship of the Book."

"Yes, the Book." Phuro said eagerly

"That is a story for another time," she said firmly. "As is the true story of the Lupe's betrayal."

"Was that how the Lexicon was lost? During that time?" Phuro asked.

"Sort of. We couldn't keep it safe. We were not safe. So the Oru Elder hid it. But many died and it was chaos for centuries. The Lexicon stayed hidden during that time but accessible until the Lupe massacred the remaining Oru in an attempt to steal the Book. But as I said that is a story for another time." She shook her head. "I wanted to show you that this standoffish attitude you've been showing is wrong."

"How do I know this story you've told me is true?" Phuro asked.

Rose merely stared at him.

He dropped his eyes.

"Why haven't you stemmed these rumors?" she asked him. "I know you've read the original translation."

Phuro kept silent.

Rose narrowed her eyes at him, and her lips tightened.

"He doesn't trust us," Hanlan told her. He had felt that from the elder Ruv many times, though there was a trace of an underlying motive, emotion.

"Humans..." she began.

"Shavora," Hanlan broke in. "He doesn't trust humans for good reason, but it's the Shavora he especially doesn't trust."

"But you seemed happy that I found Hanlan," Canin said to Phuro.

The Ruv elder remained silent, his eyes still downcast.

"He was for what it brought you. But for him I'm a headache." Hanlan looked at Phuro. "I'm the harbinger of change. And he fears that change will not be what he wants it to be."

"You do not get to choose how our fate will go," Rose told Phuro.

"And neither should he!" Phuro shouted back. "He is human!"

Hanlan got a blast of emotion from him before the Ruv controlled himself again.

"Not truly anymore," Rose said. "You either forgot or are willfully blind about what Shavora really are."

"I think it was purposefully and slowly altered over the centuries," Canin told her. "To change the feelings toward the Shavora, to leave them vulnerable."

Rose tapped her lips as a line appeared between her brow. "I think you are right," she said after a moment. "Someone wanted them assailable." She looked at Phuro. "No wonder you were not comprehensive when I took you to task about not protecting Hanlan."

Phuro was still looking at her with incomprehension. "A Ruv protects his own Shavora. They have nothing to do with the rest of the Pack."

"Shavora are gifts that encompass the whole race." She shook her head at him. "Shavora guide us to enlightenment. They keep us from turning, from the Madness."

"The individual Ruv yes." Phuro made a dismissive gesture.

"To any Ruv they touch," she corrected him. "They are lodestones. I suspect that's why the killer is fascinated with Hanlan. She can probably sense that."

"Shavora are just humans with a few of our quirks added."

"More than quirks."

Phuro made another dismissive gesture.

"You are being willfully blind." Rose shook her head at him. "I know your senses tell you how special Shavora are."

"Which is probably what scares him and makes the mistrust stronger," Hanlan told her. He had finally sorted that emotional blast he had gotten earlier and was not really surprised by what he had found.

She raised an eyebrow, clearly not understanding that.

"He doesn't like that he doesn't *know*. Things are out of his hands." She just stared at him. "He can't order things to be what he wants," Hanlan added.

"Ego?" she asked incredulously.

"Part of it is arrogance," Hanlan said. "But there is a lot of fear."

"We should be responsible for our own fate not some—human!"

"How we treat the Shavora decides our fate."

"We can't trust humans."

"Well, we can't trust our own fully either. Or have you forgotten what the Lupe did?!"

Hanlan could sense her anger and frustration at Phuro as well as Phuro's stubbornness.

"I think the misinformation has become so ingrained in us that it has become fact even to the learned like Phuro," Canin said. "What we acquire at our family's knees becomes truth no matter what we later hear."

"I'm afraid you are right." Rose looked at Phuro with something that was almost pity. "I am disappointed in you, Ulven."

Phuro got up and went into the kitchen, but Hanlan didn't hear the back door.

"I'm going to look into this," Rose said. "This is very disturbing. That someone wanted the Shavora vulnerable and the Ruv suspicious of even them."

"The Lupe may have not been the only ones who would betray the other Ruv to the Hunters."

"I fear you are right with that as well."

"Be careful," Hanlan told her. "You are one against many."

Rose met his eyes. "I will heed your warning, Shavora. But this must be corrected."

The detective felt her determination and nodded.

She rose from the chair. "If you would escort me to the door, Canin."

Canin nodded and got up from the couch. He gestured for her to proceed, then followed her into the kitchen.

Hanlan glanced at his watch and saw it was past

time for the evening news and well into prime time. He rubbed his face tiredly, then tried to relax his body. There was much he heard tonight that would take time to process.

His partner returned and rejoined him on the couch.

"We never seem to have our conversation," Hanlan said.

"I think we've had enough for the night," Canin told him.

"True enough." Hanlan sighed tiredly, but he didn't think he'd be able to sleep. Too much. He just starts to deal with stuff and more gets added. Deep thoughts, personal deep thoughts that is, were not his forte.

Canin shimmered and went wolf, laying his head across Hanlan's lap.

Hanlan gave a little laugh and started petting his partner. He knew he was being manipulated but he didn't care. Canin gave a rumbling sound and Hanlan began to relax. Maybe he would be able to sleep and with his partner guarding his slumber maybe the dreams/nightmares would stay away.

CHAPTER 16

Morning had come way too fast for Hanlan. He had finally fallen asleep around 3 a.m. but had awaken just before dawn. His partner had grumbled at him, but they both got up and did their morning routines.

Canin had made pancakes from scratch as they had time this morning and Hanlan had eaten two full plates. All that emotional stuff must have made him hungry, he decided as he drank some coffee while Canin put the dishes in the dishwasher.

The revelations of last night still lay heavy on his mind, but he pushed them aside and put his thoughts to yesterday's murders. Kezia James was spiraling. Killing those that crossed her path, not just her targets. If Deneque had been there to see

Barrington, then he was now on her radar. And possibly her next target.

"Do you know where Director Deneque lives?" he asked his partner as Canin returned to the table with two travel mugs.

"Yes." His answer was short and full of disapproval.

"We have to officially notify him of their deaths." His own voice was bland. "As we didn't last night."

Canin sighed and went to do his rounds as Hanlan got up and put his cup in the sink before picking up his travel mug at the table. The detective then went to the back door and waited for his partner.

Hanlan closed and locked the door behind them when they left. He slid into the driver's seat of the car as Canin got into the passenger side. "Where to?"

"Raven Manor. He moved in within a week of the final settlement."

"Searching for the Book, no doubt." He drove away, heading toward the Manor. "I thought Cowen would try to keep control of it."

"He is the director," Canin commented.

"Not for long if she can help it," Hanlan replied.

Canin grunted.

When Hanlan pulled into Raven Manor's circle drive, he noticed a patrol unit was parked there. It's driver's door was wide open as was the front door of the Manor. He stopped a way back from the unit. "Canin?"

"I see it."

Both of them cautiously got out of their car, pulling their weapons as they crept up toward the unit. They checked it out carefully but found nothing out of place and turned toward the front door. Keeping their weapons up, they moved slowly across the little bit of grass and concrete to the door.

"Hello? This is the police. Are you alright?" Hanlan called out as they leaned against both sides of the door.

No one answered so with a glance at each other, they slipped in to the foyer. Hanlan gestured toward the hallway and Canin nodded. They moved steadily down the hall, checking out the rooms along the way, until they came to the dining room.

The body was displayed on the table.

It wasn't Deneque as it was dressed in what was left of a police uniform. The chest was cut open and the organs were laid on the table. A slip of paper was pinned by a knife next to the head.

Sorry I missed you.

Canin pulled out his phone one-handed and called in both backup and CSU before slipping it back in his jacket.

Though the face was bruised, and swollen Hanlan recognized the officer. "It's O'Malley," he told Canin.

His partner nodded, then said, "I don't think they're still here, but we're going to stay right here until backup arrives."

Hanlan nodded in acknowledgment and lowered his gun but didn't holster it.

"What the hell?!"

At the sound of the voice both detectives whirled

toward the hallway door, bringing up their weapons.

Director Deneque stood in the doorway.

"Where have you been?" Hanlan barked out.

"At the Trust building. I've been there all night."

Hanlan studied his face. Deneque was pale, but otherwise blank-faced. He couldn't tell if the man was lying or not. No emotion leaked from him, not even fear.

Both detectives lowered their guns.

"What happened here?" Deneque asked. "How'd you get into my house?"

"We found two of your men dead in National Park last night. Canin and I came to inform you. When we got here the patrol car was here and the front door open." Hanlan spoke short and to the point. "You can see why we would need to know your whereabouts since yesterday evening."

"Several people will vouch that I was at the Trust building since yesterday afternoon."

Hanlan was sure his Hunters would, whether he was truly there or not.

Pounding came from the front door.

"That should be the officers. If you would be kind enough to let them in," Canin said to Deneque.

The director stood there a moment, then turned and went to let the officers in.

"Do you believe him?" Canin asked Hanlan.

"No. But it's possible."

Canin nodded.

Officers started to flood the doorway and Canin moved to speak with them, leaving Hanlan to brood over his thoughts alone. There were other possibilities besides Deneque being at the park.

Cowen could be involved.

"I sent them to check out the house," Canin said as he rejoined Hanlan.

"Bet Deneque didn't like that."

"No, I did not, Detective." Deneque said from the doorway. "I've already been violated once. I don't need to be again."

"We have to make sure the killer's not hiding anywhere." Canin said it as if he was repeating himself. Which he probably was.

Deneque didn't say anything, just glowered.

"Did you know Officer O'Malley?" Hanlan asked.

"No."

Canin looked at Hanlan and gave a little shake of his head, telling Hanlan he thought Deneque was lying.

"He was at the crime scene last night and now he's here. Strange coincidence," Hanlan told the Trust director.

"And that's all it is, coincidence."

The CSU arrived just then and Deneque moved away from the doorway.

Hanlan looked at the repaired wall where the secret door was and gestured to it. "You think we should check that out?"

Canin glanced at the doorway where Deneque was again standing. "I don't think he'd like that at all. He's probably standing there to make sure no one opens that door."

Deneque was glaring at the two of them.

"I'd say you were right." Hanlan glanced at the concealed door again, then shrugged. "He'll probably have his own men search it once we leave."

The two detectives drifted over to the doorway. Some of the officers Canin had sent to check out the place were returning and Canin went out into the hallway to talk to them while Hanlan leaned against the wall by the entryway.

"You shouldn't trust your partner so much," Deneque said in a low voice to Hanlan.

"I know exactly who and what he is," Hanlan told him in a just as low voice. "Just as I do you."

The Hunter looked at him sharply.

Hanlan met his eyes.

Deneque looked away first.

Canin reentered the room just then and stood next to his partner. "All clear. And Dr. Brennon is here."

"Good, then you all can clear out as soon as you remove the body," Deneque said.

"We'll need to keep an officer here to guard the scene until we can release it," Hanlan returned.

Deneque growled and stalked off.

"We can release it as soon as CSU is done," Canin told him. "Or did you just say that to annoy him."

"Mainly to annoy him." Deneque irritated him over and above his dislike of the man.

Brennon stepped into the doorway. "Detectives."

Canin gave her a nod and Hanlan greeted her with "Brennon."

"Are you about done in here, Jankins?" she called out to one of the CSIs. "I'd like to examine the body and get it out of here."

"Go ahead," the red-haired female CSI said.

"Excuse me, Detectives," Brennon said as she slipped past them, heading for the body.

The detectives watched her pull on a pair of gloves and begin her examination. She didn't take long, but Hanlan knew she had scrutinized the whole body and the displayed organs. When she stepped back, Hanlan remained by the door, but Canin went over to the M.E.

One of the morgue assistants appeared in the doorway, glanced at the table, then disappeared back down the hall toward the foyer. Probably to fetch the stretcher and more bags for the organs, Hanlan speculated. This definitely wasn't a normal pickup.

Canin rejoined Hanlan. "Consistent with being the same killer. The spleen is missing this time."

Hanlan glanced around one more time, then gestured for Canin to head out the door. "Let's go to the station. We can't do anymore here."

Canin nodded, then went through the door with Hanlan just behind him.

They headed down the hallway to the foyer where Canin paused to talk to the officer guarding the door while Hanlan continued outside. Hanlan stopped just outside the door and waited for Canin.

His partner came out a few minutes later. "I told him to keep a guard here in case IA wanted to look over the scene," Canin told him. "But if they weren't here by 1 p.m. to let the scene go."

Hanlan flashed him a smile, then they headed to the car. His partner got in the passenger side while he slid into the driver's seat. He carefully drove past the other vehicles and went out the gate before heading toward the station.

They didn't need to be long at the precinct, just long enough to fill out paperwork on this murder and to get any new information on the case. Until the BOLOs on Kezia and her brother got results they really couldn't move forward.

CHAPTER 17

Reach was off so it was Jameson who was at the evidence desk when they made it to the station. The retired officer saluted them as they went by, and Hanlan gave the older man a nod before the two detectives got into the elevator. They rode up in silence.

The bullpen was almost empty when they arrived, and they went directly to their desks. Both sat down and got to work on paperwork.

Their captain showed up an hour later as did Howell and Deneque. Captain Gardner did not look happy, and the two detectives had their poker-faces on.

Hanlan leaned back in his chair and looked at the captain.

"First, DNA came back from Davidson's apartment, and it is confirmed as Kezia James'--for the murders as well as for your 'gift'." Gardner paused. "The BOLO on Nick James' car came back this morning as well. It was found a block from your apartment."

"Came to see us and found us gone." His tone was flat, just a statement of fact. He wasn't surprised by the information. "And wanted to let us know she hadn't forgotten me."

"The autopsy reports came in last night. Brennon hand-delivered them," Howell said. "The mutilations on the face are consistent with the Ruthridge's. However cause of death is sharp force trauma to the kidneys and throat. They were choked and stabbed before the facial mutilation occurred. There were no marks on either chest."

"Their clothing had been cut open," Canin said.

"She had a time constraint," Hanlan said. "With us coming she probably wouldn't have been able to do the rest before we showed up."

"Then why cut their clothing?" Howell asked.

"To lay her hand over their heart," Hanlan told him. "To claim them."

Canin looked at him.

Hanlan felt the surge of his partner's possessiveness and protectiveness and welcomed it. He could still feel Kezia James' foul touch on his own chest.

"What's your take on this new murder?" the captain asked them. "Why is she after Mr. Deneque?"

"The books Ruthridge got at the auction were

from the AHST," Canin said, turning back to the captain. But he was still radiating protectiveness along the bond for which Hanlan was grateful.

"You still think this is all over some books?" the captain asked with a raised eyebrow.

"Yes." Hanlan nodded. "The books from the auction are the only common denominator that we can find besides Barrington's itself if we add in the Laney murders."

Deneque's cell went off and he stepped away to answer it.

"Then you're sure they're related?" the captain asked. "Kezia James would have been a baby when they happened."

"If this is a cult thing then her parents might have been members then," Canin said. "Or it might just be a family thing. We're unsure at this time."

"That was my friend Tom from Robbery." Deneque had returned, still holding his phone. "There had been a break-in at Barrington's. The auction house, not his home," he added for clarity. "Tom had heard we were looking into them."

"She obviously hasn't found what she's looking for." Hanlan frowned. "Who reported it?"

"One of the curators. She had went to retrieve an item and found the room a mess. Tom said the night guard reported no disturbances." Deneque looked upset but his voice was calm and matter-of-fact.

The captain looked at him. "You can sit this one out, Detective."

"No, Ma'am." Deneque shook his head.

She stared at him for a moment then nodded. "Alright. For now."

"Thank you, Captain." He looked at Hanlan. "You want Howell and me to follow this up?"

"Who was the curator that reported the incident?" Canin asked before Hanlan could speak.

"Mrs. Emma Wright. I did her background check. She was clean."

Canin nodded.

"You and Howell go ahead and check it out," Hanlan said. "We'll meet after lunch for an update."

Deneque nodded and he and his partner left.

"And what are you going to be doing?" the captain asked Hanlan.

"Finishing paperwork, then going back home for a few hours."

The captain raised an eyebrow.

"Until we get some forensics back we really don't have anything to do on this latest murder or a tie-in with the robbery."

"True. It would be safer here though."

"I wouldn't put it past her to slip in somehow and get me on the way to the john," Hanlan told her. "And there are plenty of places she could have privacy here."

"Point. I'm stepping up patrol in your area." She glared at him when he opened his mouth. "Or would you rather I set a car on your street?"

Hanlan closed his mouth.

"Right." She gave a nod and turned on her heel to head back to her office.

The detective watched her leave, then turned to Canin. "How much do you have to do?"

"Not much. We can leave anytime you want."

Hanlan felt a sense of urgency, but he didn't have

the information he needed. Today was the deadline that Lupo set, and he knew she wouldn't wait, would probably act early if she could, had the opportunity. Yet he was being hemmed in. Reassurance came across the bond, and he sighed before scooting back from his desk and standing. He had to get out. His gut was churning, and he couldn't sit still anymore. He just had to leave.

Canin stood as well. Concern was radiating from him.

Sliding his chair in, Hanlan glanced toward the captain's office to see her coming towards them and held in a grimace. He hoped she didn't have something else for them.

"You heading home now, Detective?" the captain asked as she stopped at Hanlan's desk.

"Yes." Hanlan kept the irritation and impatience out of his voice. "The paperwork's handled for now."

"Then get out of here."

"Thank you, Ma'am." He could feel her eyes on them as he and Canin headed for the doors. Once in the hallway, he sped up his pace and his partner kept up.

They hit the elevator and rode down in silence. Jameson wasn't at his desk, so they made the back door without distraction and hurried down the stairs. As soon as they reached the car, Hanlan slid in the driver's seat and Canin got in the passenger side. Moments later they were out of the parking lot.

"You want to stop somewhere for food?" Hanlan asked as he stopped at the stoplight just down from the station.

"No. I can heat up some soup."

Hanlan nodded and glanced in the rear-view mirror. He frowned and instead of turning right he went straight when the light changed.

They rode in silence for a few minutes, then Canin said, "We're being followed."

"You mean the black BMW with the probably illegally tinted windows or the unmarked car a few back?"

Canin raised an eyebrow.

"Why do you think I'm taking the scenic route?"

"You think the BMW is Deneque's?"

"Or Cowen's. The Trust at any rate, I think. They would now have an interest in our investigation. Of course, it could be Lupo. I make good bait."

"She wouldn't dare," Canin growled.

Hanlan harrumphed at that. Lupo didn't let little things like morals get in her way.

"Whomever the Captain assigned should get their license and name at least."

"Hopefully. If it was Howell and Deneque I wouldn't worry about that, but some of the others...Their quality of work is questionable." He was surprised some of them had made it through the academy, much less to detective, their work was so bad. Not to mention some of them were just plain lazy. Of course he suspected nepotism and family connections played a part in them getting where they were. Hanlan knew his partner agreed with him, though he didn't know the others as well as Hanlan did.

Canin grimaced, then said, "As long as it isn't Dobby and Smith." Naming the worst of them.

Hanlan grimaced himself. So he also hoped.

"This may have disrupted any plan for now, but you know it's just a delay."

The detective nodded, then slowed the car and turned into his street. He pulled into the drive and parked behind the house, but he didn't get out right away. His eyes looked past Canin, and he frowned.

Canin turned his head and stared.

There was a two-tire track between the backyards of the houses on his street and the backyards of the next streets' houses. It wasn't really a road or even an alley really, but it was there. However what held their attention was the yellow VW beadle sitting there idling.

Rose leaned out the window a bit and crooked her finger at them.

They scrambled out of their car and jogged over, then slipped into her car. As soon as the door was closed, Rose crept along the track to the one end, coming out on a cross street before speeding up.

"Is there a particular reason you're kidnapping us?" Hanlan asked, looking at her.

"You got in of your own free will," she pointed out.

Hanlan just kept looking at her with a raised eyebrow. He wasn't going to be distracted.

"The DNA results are back. It's time to set things right. No more excuses."

He knew she was talking about Phuro and his disappointing actions or really the dissatisfactory lack of such. So he was not surprised when they pulled into the Carnegie library minutes later.

Three other cars were parked along the fence and

Rose pulled next to them.

"Is it wise to meet here?" Hanlan asked her.

"The Book is here."

He nodded, then they all got out of the car and headed toward the ramp.

At the locked door, Rose did not knock but grasped the knob and turned it, opening it easily. She gestured them inside, then after following them in she closed the door firmly behind her before leading them into the library.

The seven Ruv awaiting them stared at them in surprise. Two were obviously Enforcers and of the other three strangers two were dressed in scrubs while the other looked like someone's elderly grandmother. Phuro and Gayl were the other two Ruv.

Rose went straight over to the Book with Hanlan and Canin following. She touched the lock and it unsealed, allowing her to open the cabinet. Her hands dipped in and lifted the Book out before she turned to look at the others, the Book cradled in her arms. "I am scion of Oru, one of the last so."

"Others have Oru blood," Phuro protested immediately.

"Ulven," the elderly female Ruv said in a warning tone. "Do not be decidedly dense."

Rose inclined her head to her before continuing. "Before we were Riven we were of one shape and color. After, we gained the power to become human and were shaped into a more common form but divided by coloration. Each color denoted what we were to be, something written into our very DNA by the two Gods themselves."

The elderly female Ruv looked at Rose sharply.

"Yes, I know the true story of our Rivening, Bunica. You Healers have a portion of it as do the Enforcers. The Unire is near upon us, and secrets need to be revealed. I have told the basic story to Phuro, but the rest needs to be disclosed." Rose went over to the one study table and set the Book down at the head of it. The Book's pages flipped to the front and Rose looked at the others. "Come and hear the true origin of the Ruv."

CHAPTER 18

anlan and Canin moved to the table and sat on Rose's right side while the Ruv hesitated. Then the elderly female Ruv and the two scrub-clad Ruv joined her at the table as well, settling on her left. The two Enforcers and Phuro came over but did not sit at the table, standing behind the other three Ruv.

"I am Fanpaya," the elderly female Ruv said. "This is Jarod," the male scrub-clad Ruv, "and Elsbet," the female scrub-clad Ruv. "They are scion of Loup."

Rose inclined her head to them.

Fanpaya threw a sharp look over her shoulder at the two Enforcers when they remained quiet.

"Ansel," the taller of the two Enforcers said. "Of

Vulk."

"Marcos," the other forced out. "Of Liekos."

Rose laid a hand on the Book. "There is some background that is needed before I reveal the origins of the Ruv. The supreme God, we'll call him Zeus as his name is unpronounceable in the human tongues, terraformed this planet, creating the fauna and flora and populating it with four sentient races. Zeus then left, leaving the planet in the hands of four lesser gods until he returned. One of the lesser gods left right after Zeus did, taking one of the sentient races with him. Now this is what was passed down through my family, mind you. The Lexicon itself starts after these events.

One god--we will call him Ares for ease as his name too is unpronounceable--grew bored as the eons passed with all the seeming harmony the population was having. He noticed the envy and greed a lot of the humans were feeling toward the other two sentient races and decided to nudge it along. Thus was the beginning of the fear and killing of anything that wasn't 'human' or 'normal'."

"The uncanny valley effect," Hanlan said.

"Yes," Rose nodded. "That is a remnant of it. The other two gods--we will call the one god Loki and the other Diana--tried to get Ares to undo his meddling, but he was power-mad. So they did some meddling of their own."

"The Rivening," Fanpaya said.

"Yes." Rose nodded again. "One of the reasons I'm bringing this all up is that the Hunters were once called the Children of Ares. They were more militant and vicious than their modern brethren.

Cowen is trying to bring that back," she added, looking at Hanlan. "She's part of a movement within the Hunter organization itself." Rose turned her attention back to the others. "Their main objective is to destroy us."

"Not leash us?"

"That is a more modern objective."

"You said this was one of the reasons," Fanpaya said.

"It seems there has been a systematic altering of our beliefs over the centuries. And not for the better."

"What do you mean?" Ansel glowered.

"The Shavora, for one. They are precious yet they don't get the respect they deserve."

"They're only human," Phuro growled.

"You're being deliberately obtuse again," Fanpaya told him. "They are changed by the bond. Though I think they are already different before the bond." She turned her attention back to Rose. "I had noticed a decrease in Shavora bonds over the years. You think it's deliberate?"

"Yes. They are needed just as much as you healers to keep us healthy and continuing as a race."

Phuro scowled.

"How many Enforcers have gone vigilante and rogue?" Rose asked him. "How many go Shilmulo?"

His lips tightened and he did not answer.

"When we were transformed we did not just get the good." Rose looked at him. "For everything there is a price. But the bond, the Shavora migrate that. And for more than just their Ruv."

He just stared at her with his arms still crossed.

"What is your problem?" Rose asked, frowning at him.

"He is afraid," Hanlan said, speaking up. He had been watching Phuro as Rose spoke. Not that he hadn't been listening himself, but he had sensed the turmoil of emotions within Phuro and had been keeping a eye on him in case he lost control and did something stupid.

Phuro tensed and growled, but Marcos gripped his arm before he could even think about moving. The elder Ruv snarled at the enforcer, but Marcos merely looked at him impassively.

Rose glared at him for a moment, then gestured for Hanlan to continue, her eyes still on Phuro.

"As I said before, he's afraid of the changes. But there's more than that. Rage is simmering and it's directed toward humans I believe. I feel it every time I'm around him, but it doesn't seem personal towards me." Hanlan paused as he struggled to understand what he was feeling from Phuro. This was stronger than his 'gut' that he'd always had. "It's as if he hates humans as a whole, but likes individuals. Yet is angry that he does and 'lashes out'. That's the impression I get."

Phuro glowered and crossed his arms as Hanlan talked, Marcos keeping his hand on his arm.

"Can the attitude, Ulven," Rose told him. "You have no reason to hate the human race in and of itself. The Hunters are really only a small portion of them."

"Humans are the reason we were riven, that we have to hide, that we are hunted."

"They were meddled with even as we were, though of a different type of meddling. In a way they were riven too." She studied him a bit before speaking again. "You are not betraying the Ruv by liking humans. As I said Hunters really only make up a small portion of them. Though Ares meddled with the whole race, it did not take fully with all of them. Witness the Roma. They took us in even before the Rivening."

Phuro had his jaw set stubbornly.

"If you want someone to be angry at it should be the Lupe," Rose told him. "They betrayed all of us to the Hunters. *They're* the reason we're like we are today. You condemn mankind for what they were forced to become but you ignore the Lupe for choosing to betray their own kind."

"I don't know what you mean by ignoring them. They were eradicated and eliminated as a family line for their betrayal."

"My line was thought eradicated. But what I meant was it is not spoken of as a lesson and warning. A lot of the younger generations are ignorant. I wouldn't be surprised if this alteration of beliefs could be tied to Lupe and those who were aligned with them."

Fanpaya frowned.

"Their Kumpanija and Lupus," Rose said, explaining who she meant. "Not all of Lupe's Kumpanija were made pikie. Lupus absorbed some of them."

Fanpaya's brows knitted as she continued to frown in thought. Then she looked at Phuro. "Our last Alpha, your mentor, was Lupus."

"He never spoke against humans or anything really," Phuro protested. "He let me find my own answers."

"There are many ways to lead someone to the answers you want them to find," Fanpaya told him.

"That explains a lot of things," Rose said. "Things that should not have been."

"We let a lot of things slide," Fanpaya agreed. "He was our Alpha and an Elder. And so too Ulven became. We just let it go as it seemed just little things and not worth fighting over."

Rose looked at the two Enforcers. "You allowed this to continue."

"They were our Alpha," Ansel said, meeting her eyes. "And the healers didn't protest."

Fanpaya looked distressed at this.

"That doesn't absolve you," Rose told Ansel. "Your instincts told you it was wrong, yet you allowed it."

"We are not animals to be ruled by our instincts," he told her.

She just stared at him.

"This is getting us nowhere," Fanpaya said. "We need to talk about our next moves to correct this."

"Which is part of the reason I called this meeting despite the danger," Rose said, breaking her stare and looking at Fanpaya. "We face several perils, any of which can destroy us from without or within. We need to take care of them before that happens."

"How am I destroying the Ruv?" Phuro scoffed.

Rose glanced at Hanlan, then looked at Fanpaya who gave a brief nod to tell her she got what Rose meant.

"The decrease of Shavora bonds," Fanpaya said. "More Ruv going rogue, Shilmulo."

"Due to the lack of receptiveness toward humans that Phuro has fostered," Rose agreed. "As I have said."

"Nonsense," Phuro scoffed.

"It is not," Gayl said, speaking up.

Phuro looked at her as if she had betrayed him.

She raised her chin and stared back.

"Even your protege agrees," Rose said. "You have been a detriment to the Ruv."

He stared at her with narrowed eyes. "You want me to abdicate," he said suddenly with disbelief in his voice and face.

"It would be for the best," Fanpaya said.

Phuro shot her a look, then glanced at the two Enforcers beside him but their faces were blank. He shook off the hand Marcos still had on him and stepped away from them.

"You would still be an Elder," Fanpaya told him. "Your knowledge is priceless to the Pack and the Ruv as a whole but your influence as the Alpha of the City needs to be migrated."

He turned his head slightly and stared blankly at the wall for a moment before looking at Fanpaya. "I do not agree with what has been said, but I bow to your authority in this. You could take the position away from me instead of letting me step down." Phuro straightened. "I hereby abjure my position as Alpha of the City..."

Hanlan felt something similar to relief from the Ruv elder as he spoke, but it was mixed with another emotion he didn't recognize that wasn't as dark but the same flavor as malice.

"And nominate Jami Rose as the new Alpha," he continued. He looked straight at her. "You want to change us then you can deal with the ramifications, the consequences."

"The blame, you mean," Rose said. "And you think the Enforcers will not respect me, being a female. You forget there are female Enforcers, few though they are, and they are no less capable than their male counterparts. I accept the position if Fanpaya agrees?"

Fanpaya makes the allegiance sign, fist against the heart, then opening the hand to face Rose as she swung her arm out towards her. The other five Ruv did the same and Rose inclined her head in acknowledgment.

Canin put his fist against his chest and inclined his head.

Rose returned the gesture.

Noise from the outer room leading to the main library made everyone look toward that archway. Seconds later, Director Deneque and some of his men filled the entrance.

CHAPTER 19

Most of the men stopped in the archway while Deneque and three of his men stepped inside. He frowned as he noticed Rose, then looked at Phuro. "What's happening here?"

It was Hanlan who answered. "Ms. Rose was giving us a rundown on the book we think our suspect took from Ruthridge's library."

Deneque's eyes went to Fanpaya. "And who are you? I doubt you're with the police."

"I'm the Chief Medical Examiner of the city morgue as it so happens," she told him. "Though why I'm answering you when you obviously aren't police either or invited."

"I'm actually here to warn you."

Everyone but his men looked at him with a raised eyebrow.

"My Assistant Director was planning to interrupt your meeting earlier with deadly intent. I stopped her as she exceeded her authority. However she has a strong following, and I may not be able to intercede next time."

"Why did you this time?" Fanpaya asked.

Deneque glanced at Hanlan then Rose before looking at her. "Balance is not just lip service for some of us. Nor is honor. However that doesn't mean I can't or won't do my duty." He turned and with his men went back to the archway where he looked back at Rose. "I will see you at the funeral and will-reading tomorrow?"

"Of course. That's why I'm meeting them now instead of tomorrow for this briefing about what I found out about the missing book."

"You should be careful who you associate with, Ms. Rose. It could cause you some fatal trouble."

"Like Mr. Barrington?" Hanlan asked, looking at Deneque.

Deneque just looked at him for a minute, then left, his men following him.

Gayl went into the other room behind them, then returned moments later. "They're gone," she said, remaining in the archway and keeping an eye out both ways.

Rose nodded. "The division among them is not good for either of us. But we can do nothing about that. We can however do something about the other two problems right now, especially this killer pikie. She cannot be allowed to get away with laying hands on Shavora. We must send a powerful message that Shavora are inviolable."

"And if they are the ones causing the trouble?" Phuro asked, looking at her.

"So it's my fault that Kezia James is crazy?" Hanlan said, deliberately misunderstanding Phuro's words.

Phuro ignored him and continued to stare at Rose.

"You have heard all the legends and read what little history we have retained, but you are blinded by instilled beliefs and your own stubbornness."

Hanlan could hear the pity and exasperation in her voice even without sensing it. He didn't blame her the exasperation as he felt that too toward Phuro's attitude, but he didn't feel any pity towards him. The Ruv knew his beliefs were suspect, yet he clung to them. Anger was rapidly replacing the exasperation in Hanlan though.

Canin laid a hand on Hanlan's leg and the human could feel the Ruv trying to soothe the anger.

"Get out of my way. I need to speak to Detective Hanlan."

Both Hanlan and Canin turned toward the familiar voice.

Lupo's assistant Croft was being blocked by Gayl at the archway. Every time she tried to step around Gayl the Ruv would move to block her.

"Croft, what are you doing here?" Hanlan's voice was loud enough to carry to the archway in the suddenly eerily quiet room.

The woman stopped trying to get around Gayl and looked over the Ruv's shoulder towards them.

"Julia went after James. I told her to call you, but she wouldn't listen."

"She knows where she is?" Rose broke in.

"Yes. The old textile warehouse in Alsena Heights."

"Ansel..." Rose said.

"On it," the Ruv enforcer said as he stepped away.

Rose looked at Hanlan. "I suppose you want to go."

Neither of the detectives dignified that with an answer. They merely stood.

Her eyes went then to the archway. "How did you know they were here?" Rose asked Croft.

Croft just smiled, though it was more a baring of teeth.

Rose narrowed her eyes at her but before she could say anything, Ansel stepped back up and spoke.

"I have two pairs on the way to the warehouse."

"You will go back home," Rose told Croft, looking at her with still narrowed eyes.

Croft's eyes went to Hanlan, then back to Rose before she nodded. She whirled and headed back the way she had come.

Rose looked down at the Book which began to gleam under her hand. The Book's shape began to blur and shrink until it formed a small glowing sphere. She turned her hand palm up and there was a sudden flash. When everyone's eyes cleared, the sphere was attached to a chain hanging from Rose's fingers. She fastened the chain around her neck, then slipped the sphere under her clothing. As soon as it was hidden, she looked up to see the others staring at her. "That's its original form. We didn't have a written language until we partnered with the Roma. Though we did have a rich oral language."

"The prophecy."

"It was given just after the Rivening," Rose told Phuro. "Before the Book was hidden and before we had full command of the Roma language. Human language just doesn't have the words or even some of the concepts our language had."

"As interesting as this is, we have more important things to take care of," Hanlan said impatiently. He was back in full cop mode, had been since he had heard Croft's voice, and while all this was valuable information it wasn't relevant to what they needed to do.

A text alert sounded, and Ansel looked at his phone. "The first pair's there," he said. "They're going to scout the area."

Rose nodded, then looked at Fanpaya. "We'll talk later."

Fanpaya inclined her head in acknowledgment.

"Let's go," Rose said to Ansel. She headed toward the back door with Hanlan and Canin just behind her while the two Enforcers brought up the rear.

Phuro scurried ahead of her to unlock the back door.

The detectives and the enforcers halted as Rose paused in the doorway and looked back at Phuro. "And we'll talk later too," she told him.

The Ruv elder's face remained blank.

She narrowed her eyes at him for a second before

continuing out the door, the others following suite. Phuro loudly closed and locked the door behind them as soon as they were past the doorway and Hanlan caught a small smile on Rose's lips before she schooled her face. "We'll meet you there," she told Ansel.

He nodded and the two enforcers headed for their car.

Rose looked at Hanlan. "You won't go haring off after her."

Hanlan scowled at her, shifting impatiently. They didn't have time for this. And he felt she was being unusually harsh with him. It hadn't been his fault after all that he had been captured. "Alright," he said gruffly as his partner also looked at him. "Can we go now?"

She looked at him a moment longer, then with a nod lead the way to her car. The detectives got in on the passenger side while she slid in the driver's seat. Once they were settled, she started the vehicle and backed out of the parking slot.

They remained silent the whole twenty-minute drive. Clouds had moved in during their meeting and had made it darker than normal for a fall afternoon.

The old warehouse was in shadow as lights nearest it were out. Three vehicles were parked in front of the large building, but Rose didn't park next to them. She pulled to the one side and shut off the car, laying a hand on Hanlan's arm.

Hanlan stayed and stared at the warehouse.

It was made of steel and brick mainly with two large wooden doors. There were two large-gated windows and a human-sized steel-plated door beside the wooden doors on the front. It was about two stories tall with a metal roof and overhang. Next to it was what was left of the old brick textile factory, half the building demolished. The parking lot where they sat between the two buildings was pitted and empty but for their four vehicles.

A shadow detached itself from the warehouse and Ansel glided over to their car. He leaned against her door as Rose rolled down her window. "It's quiet. Too quiet," he told her in a low voice. "The hunting pairs are inside but haven't found anything yet."

"Do you turn into a doggy too?" The words came out of the silence around them.

Hanlan tensed. That had been Kezia's voice.

Ansel turned his head and stared into the ruined factory.

Rose tightened her hand on Hanlan's arm, and he remained still and silent. She too looked toward the ruins.

A text alert sounded, but Ansel didn't move, just kept staring into the ruined factory.

Canin had transformed and was growling from the now cramped back seat, his eyes also on the ruins.

An enraged shriek rent the air, then silence again.

But Hanlan had no doubt that a fight—or at least a hunt--was going on in the ruins of the factory. Though faint, he was receiving a wealth of emotions which made that plain. Suddenly the emotions reached a peak, then just disappeared, leaving him at a loss.

Shadows moved in the ruins and then two figures appeared, dragging a struggling third. They were eerily silent as they moved closer. The enforcers finally stopped just out of reach of Ansel and their prisoner suddenly went still, her harsh breaths loud in the silence around them.

Marcus materialized from the warehouse shadows and hurried to them, carrying a set of shackles.

Kezia went crazy, striking out and twisting, but the enforcers got the shackles on her, causing her to go still again. Her loose hair obscured part of her face but didn't conceal or soften her glare.

"Was she alone?" Hanlan asked. He was sure he had felt at least six different emotional presences in the factory before they had all disappeared. And he still wasn't receiving anything from Kezia. However he was faintly sensing emotions from the enforcers, but blunted as if they were clamping down, suppressing them. Which they probably were.

"There was a male with her," One of the enforcers holding her said when Ansel gestured for him to answer.

Before anything else could be said, the other two enforcers appeared out of the factory ruins and joined their fellow Ruvs. They did not look happy.

It wasn't until she spoke that Hanlan realized that one of the new enforcers was a female. They were all dressed in bulky black coveralls with short hair and looked about the same height. There was nothing distinguishing about any of them.

"The human male got away," the female enforcer

told Ansel.

Kezia cackled.

"Find him," Ansel said simply.

The female and her partner nodded and disappeared back into the shadows.

Ansel looked back to Rose. "Alpha."

Rose released Hanlan's arm and opened her door. By the time she got out, Hanlan was out and by her side. A little smile touched her lips before she sobered and looked at Kezia.

Canin was still in wolf form and leaning against Hanlan's leg, his eyes on Kezia as well.

"Is there a chance of us being disturbed?" Rose asked Ansel.

It was Hanlan that answered though. "No. People avoid this area. Rumor has it that weird things happen here, and Patrol rarely comes here. From what I heard the few times they responded here there were 'accidents'. Twisted or broken ankles, things falling on them hard enough to bruise."

"Darane svatura," snorted one of the enforcers holding Kezia.

Kezia cackled again before saying, "Martiya. I have seen 'em." There was a tremor in her voice.

"Superstition,' the enforcer said again. "Fairy tales."

"You have caused a lot of trouble," Rose told Kezia.

The human gave her a shark's smile with lots of teeth and glistening eyes.

A Ruv in wolf form exploded out of the factory shadows and leaped towards them. But two more Ruv burst out of the shadows behind her and intercepted her, knocking her to the ground and holding her there.

"Doggy," Kezia called out, still smiling.

The Ruv renewed her struggling, trying to throw off the other two Ruv.

Rose stalked over to the struggling Ruv and smacked her across her muzzle, causing everyone to freeze in surprise.

CHAPTER 20

Everyone that is except Kezia who laughed. "Bad doggy," she blurted between laughter. The two holding her shook her roughly and she went silent.

"That is enough, Lupo," Rose growled as glared down at the female Ruv.

Lupo returned to human form and so did the two enforcers who immediately grabbed Lupo's arms to hold her still as she stood glaring at Rose. Blood matted her hair, and a bruise covered her left cheek. Any other damage was covered by her clothes.

"I am not as lenient as Ulven toward infractions," Rose told her. "You revealed our existence to a Gadji. Lucky for you she was already Marked."

"She's of the pikie," Lupo shot back sullenly.

"That doesn't excuse you," Rose returned. "Go home. Allow your companion some comfort. I will deal with you later."

Lupo glared at her for a moment longer before nodding. As soon as the enforcers released her arms, she turned and disappeared back into the factory ruins.

The enforcers nodded to Rose, then they too disappeared back into the shadows of the factory.

Rose rejoined the others.

Hanlan was still not receiving any emotions from Kezia, just getting a not-quite-right feeling about her. He could sense the alertness and contempt from the two enforcers holding her as well as Ansel's. Rose was radiating anger and contempt with an underlying fear and a bit of pity thrown in. "I suppose suggesting you turn James over to the human justice system is useless?" he asked Rose.

"Do you really think that would work?" She asked him back. "They would send her to an institution and within a few weeks she'd escape. Or even convince them to let her go. She may be crazy but there's a method to her madness as you well know."

He stared at Kezia who gazed back. A certainty hit him, and he looked at Rose. "I'll give you the escape bit, but I don't think she can fake sanity any longer. She's not all here anymore."

Rose gave him a sharp look.

Hanlan didn't know if he could explain as he didn't think there were words for what he barely grasped. "It's as if part of her left," is all he could say.

"Like a psychotic break?"

"No." He shook his head. "I'm not getting any emotions from her. She just feels—wrong. And not like a Shilmulo," he added. "I still feel emotions from them, just bad ones."

Rose frowned but before she could say anything, the two other enforcers came out of the shadows and joined the group.

"There's no sign of the male," the female enforcer said. "It's as if he vanished into thin air."

"Martiya," Kezia said again as she glanced back at the ruined factory and shuddered. "They took him away and left me for you."

Rose looked at the enforcers holding Kezia.

"She was just standing there," the one said reluctantly. "She didn't start struggling until we grabbed her and started to drag her away. But we didn't sense anyone else besides the male," he added in a confident voice. "She's just trying to spook us."

Hanlan wasn't sure about that. Rose glanced at him, and he gave her a shrug as he looked over at the ruined factory. There had been a flare of something before the emotions had all disappeared. And what had caused that?

"Take her to Fanpaya for examination. I'll deal with her later," the new Ruv Alpha added as she straightened her stance.

Ansel nodded and gestured to his enforcers before they headed toward their vehicles, dragging a suddenly struggling Kezia with them.

"I need to get you back before they realize you're gone," she told Hanlan as she turned her attention back to him.

"Too late for that. We were supposed to meet up back at the station hours ago."

She frowned at him.

"I sent a text on the way here." Canin had returned to human form. "Told them we fell asleep and to meet us at the apartment later."

"Before you went Wolfy?" Hanlan asked.

"Yes." Canin wrinkled his nose at Hanlan in distaste as Hanlan had known he would at that word. "We have forty-five minutes before they show."

"Then let's get going." Rose moved and got into the car.

The detectives joined her in the car and Hanlan waited until they were moving before speaking again. "What are you going to do with Kezia?"

"Normally judgment is decided after advisement by the healers."

"But this is different," he said as if continuing her thought.

"Yes." She paused. "There's really no choice. She has and will endanger us."

A feeling of relief went through him, making him angry at himself for that. Kezia scared him viscerally. She had had him, had claimed him, and he had felt her madness. But it was because of that madness that he was conflicted about her.

When she stopped at the next stop sign, she looked at him for a moment before driving on, her attention seemingly back on the road. "You disagree?"

"Not about the danger she poses."

"Your pity and sympathy is wasted on her."

"You pity her too," he snapped back at her tone.

"Too long among humans," she said dismissively.

But there was an underlying emotion in her words. However it was so faint he couldn't grasp it.

"John," Canin said his name softly.

Hanlan subsided and turned his gaze to the window.

Moments later, Rose flipped off the headlights and turned into the tiny track that ran behind Hanlan's apartment. She crept along for a little bit, then stopped the car.

Hanlan immediately opened the door and got out of the car.

"I'll call later," Rose said to Canin as he slid out behind Hanlan. As soon as the door was closed, she drove away.

Canin linked his arm with Hanlan and led the detective to their front door. He used his key to unlock the door and gently pushed his partner inside ahead of him. They both hung their jackets by the door and while Hanlan settled at the kitchen table, Canin headed for the coffee pot. After pouring two cups of cold coffee, he put the mugs in the microwave, then snagged the bag of donuts. He set the bag in front of his Shavora before retrieving the mugs and bringing them to the table.

Hanlan wrapped his hands around his coffee mug and stared into it.

"You need to stop expecting human reactions from Ruv," Canin told him. "We are not human."

"But I am." He looked up at his partner.

"Mmm." Canin took a sip of his coffee but didn't say anything more about that. "Howell and Deneque will be here soon."

A knock sounded on their back door as he finished speaking.

"We'll stay out here," Hanlan said as he opened the donuts.

Canin nodded and got up to answer the door.

Cold wind came in with the two other detectives. They settled at the table with Hanlan while Canin got them some coffee. Hanlan got out a couple of donuts, then offered the bag to the other two who declined.

"We just had dinner," Howell told him.

After all four were seated at the table, Hanlan spoke. "What did you find out about the burglary?"

"The items rustled through were part of the consignment from the Ruthridge estate that the Trust left," Howell said. "Stuff they didn't think their high-end clients would want."

"Tom was told only one item was missing, a clockwork medallion," Deneque added. "I got a picture of it." He pulled out his phone and tapped a few buttons before handing it to Canin. "The Curator we spoke to said it looked like a steampunk thing. None of the items had been researched, just photographed."

"Send me the pic," Canin said as he handed back the phone. "I'll study it more later."

Deneque nodded and tapped his phone again before putting it away.

Hanlan had eaten the donuts while the others were talking and was now sipping his coffee.

"Your nap doesn't look like it did you much good," Howell said to Hanlan.

"Bad dreams," was all he said to that. "Any news on the B.O.L.O.?"

"No. And nothing in the car. The captain said for you to stay home tomorrow, no going out for anything."

"I had planned on it."

"Good."

"Now that you've seen us you can tell the captain we're fine."

Howell gave him a smile, then he and Deneque stood up. "Hopefully we won't see you again until Monday."

Hanlan just grunted.

Canin got up and walked with them to the back door. As soon as they were gone, he locked the door and returned to the table. "You should eat more than those donuts."

Hanlan ran a hand over his face and gave a tired sigh. "I just want to go to bed." He didn't want to think any more. The Ruv stared at him, and Hanlan could feel his partner reach out through the bond. Comfortable warmth spread through him, and he had to struggle to not fall asleep right there in the chair.

His partner helped him up and wrapped an arm around his waist. Canin dragged him off to the bedroom and let him fall on the bed.

Kicking off his shoes, Hanlan moved around until he was comfortable and allowed himself to drift. He knew the dreams/nightmares would come. A warm body wrapped around him, and he sighed.

He probably should be protesting, but he felt so safe that he decided to worry about what he should do or feel in the morning.

His partner's rumbling pulled him down and he knew no more.

It was his partner's voice that woke him hours later.

Canin was standing in the doorway between the living area and the bedroom talking into his phone. Hanlan couldn't hear what he was saying, just his voice. But his partner wasn't happy. He could both hear and feel that.

The call seemed to end as Canin shoved his phone into its holder with extreme force and turned toward the bed. His partner then froze, telling Hanlan that the Ruv had realized he was awake.

"Who was that?" he asked as he sat up on the side of the bed and flipped on the bedside lamp.

"Jami Rose."

Hanlan could hear the reluctance in his voice that

he was radiating. "And?"

"Judgment was decided and carried out."

The human detective set his elbows on his knees, then buried his face in his hands. He dreaded the answer but asked anyway. "Did she tell you the sentence?"

"Yes." The reluctance had increased, and apprehension had joined it.

He spread his fingers a bit and looked at his partner through them when Canin didn't say anything more. The Ruv didn't want to tell him. Hanlan figured it was a case of shooting the messenger. Canin was afraid Hanlan would take his upset out on him and his partner didn't want his Shavora upset with him or upset at all.

This whole thing was making his brain hurt.

Canin wanted to comfort him but was afraid Hanlan would push him away. The human could sense that from his partner and sighed. He raised his head to look at Canin better. "Come here."

The Ruv moved hesitantly toward him then stopped two feet from the bed.

Hanlan made an exasperated noise, then grabbed Canin's arm and pulled him down onto the bed. He moved them both around until they lay spoon like on the bed with his back to Canin's chest.

"I thought you didn't like this," Canin said.

"I don't," Hanlan replied, but there was no bite or heat to the words. Truthfully Hanlan was ambivalent about this. But he knew Canin needed the contact and comfort. And if he was truthful he did too though not as much as the Ruv.

Kezia had tried to kill him. But it was her

madness that drove her to do so. He had had a glimpse of the person she could have been but for the madness. The madness had frightened him. It was a clawing thing, wanting to hook into others, almost alive. He had never felt anything like it before, not even from the serial killers he had met.

"Whatever you're thinking about, stop," his partner whispered in his ear.

Hanlan consciously relaxed his body. He had tensed up as he thought about Kezia.

Canin began his rumbling purr.

"I still don't know how you do that," he murmured. "You're not a cat."

His partner gave a rumbling laugh and increased the purring.

He lay there, dozing, his mind drifting but never fully asleep.

Canin's phone ringing pulled him fully awake. His partner rolled away and sat up to answer. "Canin...What?...We'll be there in twenty minutes."

Hanlan moved and sat up on the edge of the bed, rubbing his face. "What happen?"

"That was the captain. She says there's a break in the case and she wants us at the station now."

The human looked at his partner who didn't answer the unspoken question. Instead the Ruv headed into the living area. Hanlan got up and went into the bathroom. After a pit stop, he splashed some water on his face, then headed out into the living area himself.

Canin came out of the kitchen and handed Hanlan a slice of peanut butter toast and a cup of coffee before going back into the kitchen.

Hanlan ate the toast in a few bites, though he was not really hungry, then took a sip of coffee before following Canin into the kitchen. His partner was warming coffee in the microwave, then pouring it into their travel mugs. He could sense the Ruv didn't want to talk so he finished drinking his coffee, then put the cup in the sink. Turning, he accepted his mug from Canin before heading to the back door.

His partner closed and locked the door behind them when they left before guiding Hanlan to the car in the semi-darkness. The clouds were still covering the sky, making it seem like late night instead of early morning, and Hanlan still stumbled a bit even with Canin's aid. Hanlan slid into the driver's seat while Canin got in the passenger side.

They rode in silence, neither wanted to break the false calm before the storm that was sure to happen at the station. Hanlan parked in his normal spot, then they both got out and headed inside. No one was at the evidence room, so they continued silently to the elevator and went up to the fourth floor.

Howell was waiting for them when they got off the elevator. After a nod to them in greeting, he led them straight to the captain's office. Deneque slipped in behind them and closed the door after himself.

The captain looked at both Canin and Hanlan for a minute before speaking. "There's been a development in the case." She gestured to Deneque who handed Hanlan the large envelope in his hands. "We got a report of intruders at Officer Davidson's apartment around midnight. When uniforms responded they found the door open and that inside."

Hanlan slowly opened the envelope and pulled out the photos, apprehensive and dreading what he'd see.

The first photograph showed Kezia laying on a bed with her arms across her chest. Blood soaked her clothes and the linen around her. Her face was carved with a Glasgow Smile like her victims. The next photo showed the wall above the bed. On it was a word written in blood.

Hanlan handed the photos to his partner, then looked at the captain but didn't say anything. He was going to make her speak first.

Canin ruined that though by asking, "You think it's murder or suicide?"

Hanlan snorted as he threw a look at his partner. "Why do you think we're here, uh?"

Canin threw his own look at the captain. "You think we did this?"

"Not we, me," Hanlan said, still looking at the captain.

"You had us watched," Canin told the captain. "And Hanlan didn't leave the apartment once we got there."

A knock on the door preceded a CSI entering with a paper evidence bag and a CSU jumpsuit. The tech looked familiar, but he wasn't one Hanlan knew which told him that the captain was being serious about this.

The captain stood and ushered the others out, leaving Hanlan alone with the CSI.

After making sure the door was closed, the CSI

laid the jumpsuit on the desk and opened the evidence bag, setting it next to the jumpsuit. "I'm CSI Collins. I need you to remove your clothes and put them in the bag."

Hanlan sighed, then began stripping. He laid his weapon and holster on the desk and emptied his pockets, but everything else went into the bag.

As soon as everything was off but his underwear, the CSI stopped him from grabbing the jumpsuit. "I'm sorry, Detective, but I need to look you over." He pulled out a small digital camera and snapped a few pictures of Hanlan's upper body, especially his hands and forearms. "You can get dressed now."

"Thank you," Hanlan said dryly as he picked up the jumpsuit. He slipped it on and zipped it up before filling the pockets with his stuff. "Do you need my shoes too?"

Collins nodded and Hanlan handed him the shoes. The CSI gathered up the evidence bag and headed to the door. He opened it and left as the captain, Canin, and Howell came in.

Hanlan could feel his partner's unhappiness and anger. He wasn't very happy himself, but he knew this had to be handled seriously.

"Detective Canin, take your partner home," the captain ordered. "I'll see you both Monday."

Deneque came in then with a pair of tennis shoes and handed them to Hanlan.

"Thanks." Hanlan dropped them to the floor and slid his feet into them. He grabbed his weapon and holster off the desk, then headed out the door with Canin just behind him.

Canin waited until they were in the elevator

before he said anything. "Why you and not me? I have a reason to kill her too?"

"A version of Don't Ask, Don't Tell. You know they think we're both using each other."

"All the more reason to suspect both of us."

"Maybe. But I'm the one the Commissioner would go after." He paused as the doors opened and they got off. They walked to the back door while he continued speaking. "The captain's just covering her butt for when she gets called on the carpet for not arresting me or at least putting me on suspension."

"You going to let me drive?" the Ruv asked as they opened the door and went down the stairs.

"Nope."

"Didn't think so."

They got in the car and Hanlan turned it toward home. They were silent for a while as Hanlan drove, then he glanced at his partner. "Balance?" he asked, referring to the word on the wall.

"Crisis, judgment, would not be understood," Canin said. "At least not by humans, not even by the Hunters. But I don't think she realized the consequences of this for you."

Hanlan gave a nod of acknowledgment.

"Why would the Commissioner go after you?"

He had hoped Canin wouldn't ask. "I arrested his son last year. Junior was drunk driving and hit a homeless kid. The Commissioner thought I should let it go. I didn't and his son was fired from the prestigious law firm he had just started at. Junior was nearly disbarred but with Daddy's help he kept his license. He's a public defender now actually."

"And Daddy blames you for everything."

"Yep." Hanlan pulled into his parking spot behind his apartment and turned off the car. "Warren is not a bad commissioner, he does care about his people, but he holds a grudge for a long time."

They got out of the car and went to the apartment door. Canin unlocked it and they both went inside, closing and locking the door behind them.

"You want to eat anything?" Canin asked him.

"No." Hanlan continued on into the living area, pausing by the couch. He was physically tired, but his mind was spinning. At the station he had kept it professional but now he could feel his walls weakening.

Canin guided him into the bedroom and left him standing by the bed as he got Hanlan's sweat pants out of the dresser. He helped Hanlan undress and handed him the sweat pants.

Hanlan sat on the bed and slipped on the pants, then moved around until he was on his side. His partner spooned him, pulling Hanlan back against his chest, but Hanlan's body stayed tense.

"I know human males don't like to talk about their feelings," Canin said, his voice rumbling against Hanlan's back.

Hanlan snorted at the understatement.

"But" Canin continued. "I don't like what I'm feeling from you."

The human sighed and consciously relaxed his body. "Rose says that Shavora are valuable, but she doesn't listen or take into account my opinions. Your people have some morals and laws that go against what I think is right. While I know Kezia was dangerous, she wasn't that way purposefully, at least not of her own accord. Something twisted her. I know death was actually a mercy for her and that human treatments wouldn't have worked on her. But I can't help how I *feel*."

He hadn't meant to say all that. But the dam had broken, and he was already feeling better. Especially since Canin was nuzzling his neck and sending comfort across their bond.

"Nais," the Ruv murmured as he began his rumbling purr.

"No, thank *you*," he murmured back as he felt himself go limp. All his tension just melted away as he started to drift toward sleep.

CHAPTER 22

The rest of Sunday had been spent in bed except for pit stops to the bathroom. Canin had brought food to Hanlan a few times but had let him sleep and lounge the rest of the day away. Nobody had called.

Hanlan had gotten up early Monday morning and showered while Canin had made homemade pancakes. They had just finished eating when a knock sounded on their back door.

Canin got up and went to answer the door. He let Rose in and closed the door behind her. "Thank you for coming, Alpha."

"You said it was important."

"It is." He led her into the kitchen and gestured for her to sit at the table. Once she was seated, he spoke again. "You two need to talk. We have awhile before Hanlan, and I have to leave for work."

Rose and Hanlan just stared at each other.

Canin smacked the table, making both of them look at him. "Talk!"

Hanlan turned his eyes to Rose. "You say Shavora are important, yet you ignore or dismiss what I say because you think it's my humanness and that's not as 'worthy' as your Ruv view. I didn't think to find you as prejudice as Phuro."

"I'm not," she said with indignity in her voice and a fire in her eyes. "But we are not human, and our laws are not the same as humans'. They are harsher because they need to be."

"I get that," he told her. "But dismissing my concerns was not right either. You're the Alpha now and just dismissing someone's concerns and going ahead with your own plans is not the way to go. Not if you want your people to trust you."

The fire died in her eyes.

"I also get that you wanted to appear strong and confident to Phuro as well as the enforcers."

Rose's tense posture relaxed. "I didn't mean to devalue you. Shavora are important, especially you."

"That Prophecy again?"

"'That Prophecy' as you call it is actually part of a larger legend called The Unire where all four species reunite."

Canin's phone rang just then, and he answered with "Canin." A few minutes passed, then he said, "Alright. We'll be there in twenty then."

"The captain?," Hanlan asked as Canin put his phone away.

"Yes, we're to report to her office as soon as we get there."

"I am sorry that my actions caused you a problem with your job," Rose said as she stood. "But the end had to be as public as *her* actions."

"But it's not the end really," Hanlan told her as he stood as well. "It will be classified as an unsolved murder, not suicide, and remain open, though cold."

Rose shrugged. "But it's closed as far as her actions and motivations are concerned. The Book and Ruv are safe from prying eyes." She headed for the back door. "I will talk with you later. However I have things to do and people to see to shape the Ruv back up."

Canin had went to the coffee pot and filled up two travel mugs while the other two were talking. Now he handed Hanlan his mug, then they too headed for the back door.

Hanlan locked the door behind them, then walked with Canin to the car. He slid in the driver seat while his partner got in the passenger side. They waited for Rose to leave before they left.

"Are you angry with me?" Canin asked.

"With myself, and the situation," Hanlan told him. He should have known Canin would pick up the emotion, even though it was faint. The talk with Rose had settled some of his emotion, but some anger still hovered. Relief flared in Canin, and Hanlan glanced at him. "The talk was a good idea. Though you should have said something to me first. I don't always react well to surprises."

Canin gave a nod of acknowledgment. But not

one of agreement, Hanlan noted.

Moments later they were at the station and Hanlan parked in his usual spot. They hurried up the stairs and into the building.

Reach was at the evidence desk and waved them over.

"I guess you heard," Hanlan said as they stopped at the window.

"About a lot of things. I've been keeping my eyes on the Trust, especially on Cowen. She's Trouble with a capital T."

Hanlan looked intently at Reach for a moment. "You wouldn't happen to know anything about her exceeding her authority the other day, would you?"

Reach gave them a little smug grin.

"Just be careful," Hanlan said.

"Of course." Reach looked offended.

"We need to get upstairs," Canin said with a nod toward the elevator.

Reach waved them away and they headed to the elevator. They rode up in silence and when the doors opened Howell was waiting for them. The three of them went into the bullpen and walked over to the captain's office.

Deneque and the captain were waiting inside, and Howell closed the door behind them after the three of them entered.

"The lab didn't find any blood on your clothes or anything that would put you at the crime scene," the captain said. "Plus the surveillance car said you didn't leave once."

"I'm sure that didn't make the Commissioner happy," Hanlan replied.

"No." The captain grimaced. "Palamar and Duncan are assigned the case."

"Not them?" Hanlan waved his hand toward Howell and Deneque.

"They're to assist, but the Commissioner wanted an unbiased pair of detectives to investigate."

"And you chose those two?" Hanlan asked incredulously.

"Well, they were sort of involved anyway," the captain said with a small smile. "They were the surveillance team."

"Ah."

"So finish your paperwork for this case, then get back to your others. You'll be back on rotation tomorrow."

Hanlan threw her a sloppy salute, then turned on his heel and headed for the door with Canin just behind him. Howell opened the door for him, and he sailed through, Canin following. As soon as they got to their desks, Hanlan dropped into his chair and sighed. They had just dodged a big bullet.

Canin sat in his own chair and got onto his computer immediately.

Hanlan could feel the satisfaction radiating from his partner. They were back to doing what they were meant to do or at least what they wanted to do, catching mundane murderers. No world-ending fate resting on their shoulders, just the fate of a single murderer or murderers.

Turning his chair, Hanlan got on his own computer and began the mountain of paperwork that awaited him.

ABOUT THE AUTHOR

This is the second book in the Ghostwolf Series. Books in the Ghostwolf Series are set in our contemporary world where the Del Mulanti Ruv, Ghostwolves, are hidden among us. Book 1, Raven Manor, is available on Amazon and Kindle Unlimited. Raven Manor is actually more of a prequel than an actual book 1, setting up the events for this book. Check it out.

If you have enjoyed this book, then please leave a review to help other readers to experience the joy. Also Authors love feedback.

I have an email list. If you wish to join go here: https://mailchi.mp/27d0cd719a63/tls-grimoire

Or if you just want to see what I'm doing go to my main blog at https://tlriffey.blogspot.com

9 781956 806588